"I must have more time to think," Fiona said.

"There is no time," Ian replied. "The future of Craighill must be settled now. If words won't convince you, perhaps this will!"

Fiona barely heard him through the pounding of her heart as his fingers moved from her shoulder to the whiteness of her throat. Her chin was cupped in a cool hand that had a touch of fire.

In spite of herself she moved toward him, driven by such a strong urge to touch him that she was afraid...afraid of the new sensations sweeping through her.

How could she marry Ian on the basis of a business arrangement when she knew now, and for all time, that he was the man she loved? And Ian had made it clear that he wanted only Craighill, not her....

WELCOME
TO THE WONDERFUL WORLD
OF *Harlequin Romances*

Interesting, informative and entertaining,
each Harlequin Romance portrays an appealing
and original love story. With a varied array
of settings, we may lure you on an African safari,
to a quaint Welsh village, or an exotic Riviera
location—anywhere and everywhere that adventurous
men and women fall in love.

As publishers of Harlequin Romances, we're
extremely proud of our books. Since 1949,
Harlequin Enterprises has built its publishing
reputation on the solid base of quality and
originality. Our stories are the most popular
paperback romances sold in North America; every
month, six new titles are released and sold at
nearly every book-selling store in Canada and the
United States.

A free catalogue listing all Harlequin Romances
can be yours by writing to the

HARLEQUIN READER SERVICE,
(In the U.S.) M.P.O. Box 707, Niagara Falls, N.Y. 14302
(In Canada) Stratford, Ontario, Canada N5A 6W2

We sincerely hope you enjoy reading
this Harlequin Romance.

Yours truly,

THE PUBLISHERS
  Harlequin Romances

The Master of Craighill

by

SHEILA STRUTT

Harlequin Books

TORONTO • LONDON • NEW YORK • AMSTERDAM
SYDNEY • HAMBURG • PARIS • STOCKHOLM

Original hardcover edition published in 1979
by Mills & Boon Limited

ISBN 0-373-02333-2

Harlequin edition published May 1980

CHAPTER ONE

FIONA MONTROSE turned the car in through the tall stone gateposts and edged her way carefully along the pitch-dark drive to Craighill. In just a few minutes now she would know what sort of reception awaited her when she arrived to claim her inheritance. Her sudden jolt of apprehension had nothing to do with the bumpy gravel under the wheels.

Sensing that they had reached the end of their journey, Bowser slowly came to life on the seat behind her. It had been a long day's drive from London to the Border country of Scotland and, cramped after his confinement, the big dog shook himself— and the car.

The drizzling rain that had made the last stage of the journey through the switchback hills of the Cheviot Hills such a nightmare had stopped, but there was no moon. It was still hidden behind massed banks of cloud, leaving the laurel bushes lining the drive as no more than shiny black outlines against the threatening March sky.

Strained from the effect of peering through the smeared windscreen, Fiona's eyes felt as though they were bursting from her head by the time she finally rounded the last curve in the mile-long approach and the bulk of Craighill House reared up in front of her. There were no lights in the windows and the house stood there as a menacing presence, only slightly darker than the surrounding darkness.

Fiona switched off the engine. Except for the rapid ticking of hot metal, there was total silence. Nothing, not a sound, not a movement, disturbed the overall stillness. She opened the door and Bowser scrambled across her and jumped out, glad to be away. Fiona got out more slowly, gratefully aware of the rain-fresh country air on her face as she walked round to the front of the car and stood in the pool of light thrown by the headlamps.

The noise of Bowser wuffling enthusiastically in the nearby shrubbery only served to intensify her sense of total isolation. She could not see the dog, and when she heard the deep warning growl in the back of his throat that he used to announce the approach of strangers, she could feel the hair literally rising on the nape of her neck.

Footsteps came scrunching towards her across the gravel, frightening in the darkness lapping the edge of the pool of light in which she stood. Bowser barked and was answered by a firm masculine voice. The dog whined and then the scratching of his paws joined in with the approaching footsteps of the unknown stranger.

By the time the tall figure of a man had reached the edge of the circle of light, Fiona was at screaming pitch. He stood for a second, looking at her.

'Good evening,' he said. 'You'll be Miss Montrose, no doubt.'

The voice was deep, well modulated, with scarcely a trace of Scottish accent, and Fiona had the impression that its owner was only too aware of the pitch of near-hysteria that she had reached during those few moments alone in the darkness, listening to his steadily approaching footsteps. Aware and, if anything, slightly amused at her unwarranted fear.

Struggling to keep any sign of a tremor out of her voice, Fiona forced herself to reply with all her newly acquired authority as mistress of Craighill.

'Yes, I'm Fiona Montrose,' she said. 'And who are you?'

'Ian Hamilton, at your service,' came the reply.

'But you can't be!' The words were out before Fiona could stop them, all fear replaced by total amazement.

The square-set, middle-aged man she had pictured in her mind's eye whenever she had thought about Craighill's estate manager had been nothing like the tall, dark figure now standing in front of her. Not only was Ian Hamilton disconcertingly handsome but, worst of all, he could certainly not be more than thirty.

She was very aware of his long, cool scrutiny, which had a hint of hostility in the unwavering eyes. And that, she told herself, would hardly be surprising. She had, after all, taken Craighill away from him.

In her discomfort, she spoke more sharply than she had intended.

'How do you do?' She held out her hand, noticing that his lips had set into a thin line. His grip was firm but formal, almost impersonal, and the eyes that held her own forced them to drop before he turned and waved a casual hand in the direction of the still-darkened house.

'This is a poor welcome for you,' he said evenly. 'Macbeth should have put the front lights on. We only use the back of the house—that's why she didn't hear you. I'll give her a touch of the horn.'

He moved away from the circle of light and in the second before the car horn blared out behind her, Fiona wondered about the dramatically named Macbeth. Then the entrance lights sprang on and a tiny woman was standing outlined in the open doorway.

'I'll take your arm—the footing's not too good.' The touch of his hand on her elbow made Fiona jump. She had not heard him return to her side. 'We'll get you indoors and then I'll come back for your luggage.'

'There's no need for you to do that!' Fiona attempted to withdraw her arm, but the fingers merely tightened and, whether she liked it or not, she was led up the steps towards the figure waiting for them.

'Miss Montrose—welcome to Craighill!' The tiny, middle-aged woman spoke in an accent that even Fiona, brought up in the south of England, had no difficulty in recognising as coming from the heart of Glasgow. 'I'm Janet Macbeth, Sir Hector's—I mean, your housekeeper. The lawyers said to stay on anyway until you'd made up your mind——' She began her explanation with them standing on the step in front of her until a look from Ian Hamilton stopped her in her tracks. 'What am I thinking of, gossiping on while you're outside in the cold and wet?' she said apologetically. 'Come in, come in!'

She stood to one side so that Fiona could walk past her into an immense hallway going way up into the shadows in the roof. It struck chilly with disuse and Fiona was craning her neck, taking in the wide carved staircase, when Janet trotted past her.

'If you'll follow me, Miss Montrose,' she said, 'we'll soon have you warm and a good meal inside you.'

She headed off towards the darker shadows at the back of the hall. Following her and listening to the echo of her footsteps on the marble floor, Fiona realised that both the scratch of Bowser's paws and the firmer tread of Ian Hamilton were missing. The estate manager had gone back to the car to get her luggage after all, she supposed, and Bowser must have gone with him, but she was suddenly too tired to care. Tired, wet and physically and emotionally exhausted by the long drive and by the moments of sheer nerve-tingling fright when she had listened to the unknown footsteps coming towards her out of the night.

'This way, Miss Montrose.' Janet was holding

open a green baize door under the stairs at the back of the hall.

Fiona went through and found herself in a new world of light and warmth, a world in which the appetising smell of cooking was mixed with just the faintest hint of beeswax polish. The kitchen in front of her was a medley of scrubbed pine and glowing copper. Rush mats lay on the floor to take the chill out of the grey stone flags and a huge old-fashioned range stood in the open fireplace. The presence of a modern electric stove indicated that the range was no longer used for cooking, but it was still black-leaded until it shone and a fire glowed brightly behind its bars. Fiona moved gratefully into its circle of warmth.

Janet was still chattering on, her heavy nasal accent difficult to understand at times.

'We've lived in the servants' quarters for a good long while now,' she said. 'Your uncle as well—God rest his soul,' she added, instinctively pointing to a well-used armchair by the side of the range. 'The old laird was not a man to spend a penny on a house that had only three people in it unless he had to! But it's comfortable enough, and the young master said to leave everything as it was until you'd decided. . . .'

Janet continued to ramble on, but Fiona was no longer listening. The young master! The title indicated more clearly than any other words that, having grown up as her great-uncle's foster-son, Ian Hamilton had indeed expected to inherit Craighill. The situation was likely to be even more difficult than she had anticipated in her worst moments in London, she thought gloomily.

'.... but mebbe you'll be wanting to change it yoursel'?' Janet stopped talking and looked at Fiona expectantly.

'What? Oh, yes, maybe!' Although Fiona had not heard the whole question, an answer was clearly required. 'But for now, Mrs Macbeth....'

'*Miss* Macbeth,' the voice corrected her. 'Janet.'

'Well, Janet, then!' Fiona smiled down at the tiny housekeeper. 'Well, for now, Janet, what I'd like to change most would be these clothes!' She gestured down at her suit. Damp from the time she had spent waiting in the soaking wet drive, the cuffs of the trousers were now beginning to steam slightly in the heat from the fire.

'Oh, and me chattering on with you so wet and all!' Janet said contritely. 'My tongue'll be the death of me! Long enough to hang a week's wash on, my old mother used to say!'

Still talking nineteen to the dozen, she opened a door at the back of the kitchen and led the way up a steep and narrow flight of poorly lit stairs. A shadow fell across them as they reached the top, and unaccustomed to her new surroundings, Fiona jumped, cross with herself the moment she realised that it was Ian Hamilton standing to one side to let them pass. Even before she could smile her thanks, he had started down the stairs. 'Your luggage is in your room,' he said shortly.

He disappeared into the lighted kitchen and Janet looked after him.

'It'll be difficult for the young master,' she said sympathetically.

A few steps further along the barely carpeted passage, she stopped and opened the door into a big, old-fashioned bedroom.

'This was the old laird's room,' she explained. 'The young master said for you to have it, but if you would prefer somewhere else. . . ?' The Glaswegian accent trailed away and Fiona looked round the high-ceilinged room with its somewhat overpowering assortment of heavy Victorian furniture.

'No, this will do splendidly,' she said, noticing that a bowl of daffodils had been placed on the mahogany dressing table to brighten the room and maybe to lay any suspicion of ghosts. But for her there were no ghosts. She had been acting on an impulse that she barely understood when she had answered an advertisement in the personal column of *The Times* asking for possible surviving kin of the late Sir Hector Montrose to contact a firm of London solicitors. Until then she had never known that she had had a great-uncle of that name; far less that he had been a person of considerable wealth and property on the Borders of Scotland.

Replying to the advertisement had started a chain of events that still amazed her. She had discovered

that her grandfather had been Sir Hector's younger
brother, but with her grandfather and her father
both dead, Fiona had been the only relative left to
inherit Sir Hector's estate of Craighill.

Now, standing in his house with his housekeeper
at her side, the only feelings she had for her late
great-uncle—the old laird, as he was apparently
called up here—were of gratitude mixed with a certain sympathy for a man who had been unable to
leave his property as he undoubtedly would have
wished.

The solicitor had gone to great lengths to explain
that the estate had been entailed; legally bound to
be inherited by the next surviving relative. The
solicitor had also made it clear that if Sir Hector had
been able to have his way, Craighill and everything
that went with it would have been left to the man
who had been brought up as his foster-son—Ian
Hamilton, the man who had greeted her on arrival
and who had now just passed them so frigidly on the
stairs.

'No, this room will do splendidly.' Reminded of
the housekeeper standing patiently by her side,
Fiona broke her chain of doleful thought and in-
jected a note of brightness into her voice that she
certainly did not feel. 'And thank you for the daffodils,' she added.

'Aye, well, it's a small enough thing.' Janet
smiled, evidently pleased nevertheless that her gesture had been noticed.

'And I hope that you'll stay on as my house-keeper,' Fiona added.

When a beaming Janet had finally closed the door, Fiona went through into the bathroom leading off the bedroom and turned on the water. A hot bath might relax her, she thought, hunting for her dressing gown in the luggage that Ian Hamilton had left at the foot of the big, old-fashioned bed. Although Janet might be willing to accept her, the estate manager's attitude so far had been even more intimidating than she had feared. Fiona sighed. There was no doubt that the situation at Craighill was going to be as difficult and complex as she had anticipated in her worst moments in London.

It would not have been so bad if the man she had unwittingly disinherited had not been quite so different from what she had imagined.

When the solicitor had passed on the rumour which had circulated the district that the estate manager and foster-son, Ian Hamilton, might actually be his natural son, Fiona had jumped to the conclusion that he would be a man in his fifties. After all, the old laird had been well into his eighties when he had died and any son of his, Fiona had reasoned, was bound to be well into middle age.

The picture that had formed in her mind's eye had been of a square-set, grey-haired man with a grown-up family and too settled in his ways to want to move away from Craighill even though the estate that he had grown up expecting to inherit had been so suddenly taken away from him. Obviously there would be difficulties, but Fiona had felt somehow confident of her ability to deal with them. Maybe she would even be able to make friends with a man who would be old enough to be her father. Maybe he might even come to take the place of the father who had been killed in a road accident fifteen years earlier, when Fiona was seven.

Now that she had met him, the thought of turning the tall, hawklike young man who had greeted her arrival into a father figure was so fantastic as to be quite laughable—if only it had not been quite so daunting. There was something about the Ian Hamilton of flesh and blood, rather than the person of her imagination, that made it clear that here was a man accustomed to command. A man who was not going to relinquish his authority over Craighill just because Fiona herself happened to be the legitimate heir.

A gurgling noise from the pipes made her remember her bath and she caught the piping hot water just as it was coming to the rim.

She delayed going downstairs as long as she could, studying the faded photographs on the walls while she dressed. They spoke of happy times long past in her great-uncle's life, and one girl's face in particular appeared again and again. She was in the middle of a long train of speculation about why her great-uncle had not married when she realised that it was getting late and that she could put off her second confrontation with his estate manager no longer.

She went downstairs and steeled herself to meet the first glance from those raking, hostile eyes as she opened the kitchen door. Her precaution was unnecessary. Janet was at the stove, but otherwise the kitchen was empty. There was no sign of Ian Hamilton.

'You'll be ready for your supper, Miss Montrose.' The housekeeper ladled soup into a plate and took it to Fiona's place at the table. 'The solicitor's letter said you were coming today, but he didn't say exactly when you'd be here, so I made a game pie with this soup to warm you first. We have all our meals in the kitchen,' she added.

Looking at the cold pie on its dish in front of her, golden-brown crust fluted and tempting, Fiona knew that, whatever problems might be ahead of her, Janet's cooking was not going to be one of them. She lifted the steaming soup spoon to her lips and then stopped.

'Janet, where's Bowser?' she asked, looking round the kitchen.

'Who?' The housekeeper was clearly perplexed.

'Bowser—he's a dog. I brought him with me and when I last saw him, he was out in front with Mr Hamilton.'

'Then he'll be safe enough in the kennel in the yard. There's no need to bother yourself,' Janet said reassuringly as Fiona began to get up from the table, guilty about having forgotten Bowser for so long.

'He'll be fine. The young master will have fed him.'

'But Bowser's an indoor dog—I mean, he's always lived indoors,' Fiona explaind. 'I can't possibly leave him outside all night. If you'll tell me where the kennel is, I'll go and get him.'

'It's through the back there.' Janet pointed an uncertain finger. 'But I don't know that the young master will. . . .'

What Janet did not know was to remain a mystery. Fiona went through the back door and out into the night. She stood for a second, letting her eyes adjust themselves to the sudden darkness until the darker shapes of the barns and outbuildings began to materialise and a dog kennel became visible just a few yards away.

All was silence as she approached, but then there was a rustle of straw and a suspicious-looking Bowser appeared at the end of a length of chain.

'Here, boy!' Fiona called. 'Did I forget all about you, then?'

The heavy tail began to wag delightedly but, frustrated in his efforts to jump up by the chain attached to his collar, the big dog sat obediently as Fiona wrestled with the clasp.

'What are you doing, woman?' The quiet voice came authoritatively out of the darkness at her shoulder.

Startled as much by the mode of address as by his silent approach, Fiona spun round and came face to face with her estate manager.

'I'm getting Bowser,' she said, wondering why he made her feel so much on the defensive.

'To take into the house?'

'That's right.' Fiona bent down and tried again to undo the stubborn catch.

'But he's perfectly all right where he is.' Ian Hamilton's voice expressed no doubt.

'That's as maybe.' Fiona wished she did not have to continue their conversation from the disadvantage of her ridiculous half crouching position, but the clasp on Bowser's collar seemed determined not to give way. 'But Bowser has always lived indoors and I'm certainly not going to leave him out here— alone—on his first night in a strange place!'

'Oh, I see.' There was a hint of sarcasm in the estate manager's voice.

Spurred on by the sarcastic smile that she had no doubt was on the face above her, Fiona redoubled her efforts, only to be rewarded by the clasp and Bowser parting company with a suddenness that sent her reeling back, and had it not been for Ian Hamilton's hand coming out to steady her, she would have fallen.

Damn, damn, damn! she thought as Bowser, just to make the situation worse, made frantic efforts to come between them and lick her face.

'Get down!' Ian Hamilton spoke sharply, and surprised for once into obedience, Bowser backed away.

Only too aware of her paw-marked sweater and

flushed and shining face, Fiona did her best to ignore the sardonic smile showing itself in the gleam of white teeth on a level with her eyes.

'Before that great lapdog of yours does any permanent damage,' he said in a voice that made her feel about twelve years old, 'I think I'd better see you both safely inside.'

Without waiting for a reply, he took her firmly by the arm and led her back towards the house, Bowser following at their heels. He opened the back door and in the light that streamed from the empty kitchen Fiona could see that he was once more deadly serious.

'If you take my advice, Miss Montrose,' he said, 'you'll be careful about allowing that animal to run free. You're on a farm now, with livestock about, and there's no knowing what harm he might do.'

Before she could protest about his high-handed manner, the pressure on her arm was gone and Fiona was listening to his footsteps disappearing into the night.

CHAPTER TWO

THERE had been no further sign of Ian Hamilton that night. Smarting under the way in which he had treated her, Fiona had been childishly determined to have her own way. She had taken Bowser to her room and the last thing she had been aware of before she had fallen asleep had been the dog's weight resting heavily on her feet.

When she woke, the sun was streaming into her room. Braving the chill, she threw open the window and leaned out into the clear March morning. The only sounds were the distant cawing of rooks and the bleating of sheep—so different from the constant street noises that she had heard every morning in the mews house that she had rented in London.

The barnyard beneath her window that had been a place of eerie dark shadows the night before now proved to be an immaculately kept stretch of gravel, flanked by barns and outbuildings. This was her first full day in residence as mistress of Craighill and suddenly, superstitiously, she was determined to let nothing spoil it.

Even Bowser co-operated. After a quick run in the yard, he went and lay down quietly in a corner of the kitchen and buried his black nose in his paws.

The table was set for two people and Fiona was already sampling her first Scottish breakfast of porridge and thick cream, followed by bacon and eggs and home-made bread and marmalade, when a brief 'Good morning!' announced her estate manager's arrival.

'Good morning.' Fiona watched from under lowered lashes as Ian Hamilton washed and dried his hands at the sink in the corner. There was no way of telling, but she hoped that he too had decided to forget the underlying friction between them the previous night and make a fresh start.

He cocked an eye in Bowser's direction, but he said nothing and his thoughts were still a mystery as, with Janet hovering round him like an anxious mother hen, he sat down and began his breakfast.

Watching him eat, Fiona got the impression that he had already been hard at work and that her own eight o'clock start to the day was late by the standards of Craighill. She would get up earlier in future, she promised herself.

'Do you ride, Miss Montrose?' he asked suddenly.

'Ride? Oh, yes, I love it, as a matter of fact.' Fiona immediately thought of Blue Fire, the dapple grey thoroughbred she had left with friends on the outskirts of London until she could bring her to Scotland. Blue Fire would love it at Craighill, she thought, looking up with a smile to find his eyes studying her.

'It's good that you ride,' he said, 'because the best

way to see Craighill is on horseback. If the idea appeals to you, I thought we might beat—that is, ride round—the boundaries today.'

'That would be wonderful.'

'Then I'll meet you in the yard about ten. I'll tell Sim to have the ponies ready—and that'll mean two packed lunches as well, Macbeth,' he added casually to Janet at the stove.

Janet beamed, apparently not in the least put out by his offhand manner. He had taken control again, Fiona realised, but this time she was determined not to let it bother her. Instead she distracted herself by studying him as he sat there calmly eating his breakfast.

Seeing him for the first time in the bright light of day Fiona realised that the eyes she had thought of as brown the previous night were, in fact, grey; a very dark grey, shading almost imperceptibly away from the black pupils. His hair, too, was black, curling crisply down into the nape of his neck, and the eyelashes that shadowed his cheeks as he bent over his plate would have been the envy of any woman.

But the eyelashes were the only delicate thing about him. Otherwise the face was strong, even hawklike. The rather straight, thin lips added a touch of ruthlessness redeemed only by the tiny laughter lines at his eyes. Although it was the end of winter, his skin had the permanent, even tan that comes with spending long hours out of doors and the unbleached yarn of his Arran sweater accentuated the tanned face, making it seem darker than it really was.

The thought of spending the whole day alone with him brought an irrational sense of trepidation. She had already felt the latent strength of his fingers gripping her arm and he was tall, well over six feet. Five feet eight herself, Fiona rarely had to look up to meet the eye of any man, but the previous night she had had to tilt her head way back to match the level scrutiny of Ian Hamilton.

At that moment, in the way she had already learned that he could catch her unawares, he looked up. It was evident that he knew she had been studying him. Fiona was scarlet with embarrassment as he stood up and towered above her.

'If you'll excuse me,' he said, 'there's an hour's work waiting to be done before I meet you with the ponies in the yard, Miss Montrose.'

'Fiona, please!' She spoke impulsively and regretted it an instant later.

He paused, 'Aye, Fiona then,' he said flatly, and then he was gone, the draught of cold air set up by his departure lingering in the warm kitchen.

Piqued by his lack of response to her overture of friendship, Fiona sat back in her chair and fumed. If *Mr* Ian Hamilton wanted to keep their relationship on a purely formal footing, it was all right with her!

'Shall I be showing you the house?' Janet broke into her train of thought and Fiona looked up to see the tiny housekeeper poised expectantly at her side with a tray of dirty dishes in her hands.

She considered the offer.

'No, not now, Janet,' she decided. 'There's not really enough time to do a great place like this justice before I go riding with Mr Hamilton,' she went on, but the housekeeper looked crestfallen, and the last thing Fiona wanted was for her to feel as rebuffed as she herself had felt a few seconds before. Unlike Mr Ian Hamilton, she had no wish to antagonise people who were prepared to be friendly. She tried a tentative smile and was pleased to see the houskeeper's face brighten. 'I want to give you lots of time when you take me round, so for now I think I'll just take Bowser for a walk and have a look at the outside.'

Bowser had been dozing, but at the mention of his name he got to his feet and began yelping expectantly. Fiona could still hear him when she was upstairs getting her coat.

She could just imagine Janet's reaction to the noise. Bowser really was getting her into trouble, and it was ironic when he was not even her dog.

Bowser belonged to Geoff Gilson, a young civil engineer who had rented her his mews cottage in the fashionable London district of Kensington very cheaply on condition that she take care of the dog. Geoff had gone off to Africa on a bridge-building contract and the only thing that had bothered him was who would look after Bowser while he was away.

Fiona had promised, and she had kept her promise, bringing the shaggy animal to Scotland rather than putting him in kennels.

She flung on her coat and hurried downstairs to rescue Janet from the noise. The dog leaped at her the moment she opened the door, but Janet stayed where she was; at the kitchen table, buttering rolls, her shoulders hunched in an attitude of extreme disapproval.

'We'll be off now, Janet,' Fiona said wheedlingly.

The housekeeper did not look up. 'And not before time!' she said crossly. 'The one thing the old laird would never allow was a dog in the house!'

With an inward shrug, Fiona opened the door and Bowser shot out, nearly knocking her over in his eagerness to be away into the bright, crisp morning.

He disappeared at speed around the corner and, following more slowly, Fiona walked along the side of the house to the front. The doorway, the gravelled drive and, above all, the evergreen shrubbery that had seemed so menacing the night before when the sound of Ian Hamilton's footsteps had been coming towards her through the darkness looked quite different in the morning light. Her car had gone, she noticed, presumably garaged in one of the outbuildings at the back.

Even craning her neck, the house was so big that she could see very little. Giving Bowser a shout, she left the path and began to walk through the shrubbery in the general direction of the drive, hoping that if she got further away, she would have a better view. The grass crackled under her feet and the glossy green laurel leaves were still edged with the faintest hint of early morning frost. Fir trees stood black against the pale March sky and the distant cawing of rooks came clearly through the still morning air.

The peace of the countryside that Fiona remembered from her childhood in Kent settled about her shoulders like a well-fitting cloak, making her more pleased than ever that, against everyone's advice, she had decided to come north and live in her inheritance. She stepped off the grass on to the drive and turned to face the house.

The house and the estate were both called Craighill and the house was set in a hollow, protected from the north winds by clumps of tall fir trees. The distant tops of the moorland rolled away in the distance, but it was the house rather than its setting that claimed Fiona's full attention. It was huge, more like a small turreted castle than a home. Grey stone walls soared up towards a medley of darker grey slate roofs. The front door was set at the foot of a circular central tower, forming the apex of an inverted vee from which the building swept back in two distinct wings. Unevenly spaced windows made it difficult to guess how many stories there were, and there were also tiny barred windows huddled up underneath the steeply pitched roof.

Looking at its vast bulk and at the many smokeless chimneys rising up into the sky, Fiona could understand why her uncle had chosen to live in the servants' quarters. Craighill would obviously cost a fortune to heat and maintain and, for a man on his own, the days of country life on such a grand scale were long past.

She walked slowly back along the side of the house towards the yard. Even Bowser must have been cowed by the sheer size of the place, she thought, because for once he was walking to heel. She looked at him. He had already upset Janet once that morning and as she would be gone for the whole day, it seemed wisest to tie him up. It went against the grain, but there was no sense in antagonising Janet by leaving a noisy, boisterous dog in the house. Ian Hamilton's slightly superior attitude was quite enough to cope with for one day.

Bowser barked reproachfully when Fiona left him in the kennel, straining at the end of his chain.

'Can't be helped, old boy!' she called back over her shoulder as she went into the house.

There was no one in the kitchen, but two ready packed knapsacks stood on the table. Fiona glanced at her watch. She had been out looking at the house longer than she had intended and she would have to hurry if she was not to put herself at the further disadvantage of keeping her reluctant escort waiting.

She was back in the kitchen within five minutes. Her long legs looked even longer in cream twill riding breeches and boots and she was quite unconscious of the effect that the blue polo-necked sweater under her tweed hacking jacket had in intensifying the unusually deep blue of her eyes. Although it seemed strange to be going riding without its protection, she had decided against wearing her hard, velvet-covered jockey cap. Sensing that Ian Hamilton might find it faintly amusing, and unable to face yet another one of his sarcastic smiles, she had substituted a gay silk scarf instead.

The kitchen was still empty, but someone had been there in her absence and taken the two knapsacks. Their disappearence meant that Ian Hamilton was probably ready and Fiona had to resist the temptation to half run out of the house in order not to keep him waiting.

Her estate manager was indeed waiting for her. He was in the far corner of the yard talking to a small, thickset man, dressed in the heavy clothes of an outdoor worker and holding the reins of two sturdy fell ponies. The knapsacks were already strapped to the saddles and, abandoning her good resolution, Fiona hurried towards them. At the sound of her quick footsteps, Ian Hamilton looked up.

'Ready? Good!' He waved an arm to encompass them both, but his smile was more for the old man at his side. 'Here she is, Sim. Here's the new owner you've been waiting to see. The old laird's great-niece, Miss Fiona Montrose.'

'Hallo, Sim.' Fiona held out her hand.

The man ignored it and instead looked up at her with suspicion deeply embedded in his dark brown eyes. After a few seconds, he turned back to Ian Hamilton, leaving Fiona both mortified and at a loss.

'She's awful young,' he said.

'Aye, but time'll change that,' Ian replied.

Unused to being discussed as if she had not been there, Fiona shifted uncomfortably, and to her surprise Ian came to her rescue.

'Give her the pony, Sim,' he said.

The awkward moment passed as Fiona took the reins from the gnarled, weatherbeaten hand that held them. She could feel Sim's eyes boring into her back as she checked the girth and then swung herself lightly into the saddle. With an expressionless face, the old yard man handed the reins of the second pony to Ian.

'Mebbe it'll not be so bad,' he said before he stumped off away from them across the yard.

'Are they all like that?' Heartened by Ian's support a few seconds earlier, Fiona could not resist the question.

He swung himself competently into the saddle. 'Like what?' he asked, thigh muscles flexing against the tight cloth of his breeches as he adjusted the stirrups to his long legs.

'Full of quaint old-fashioned charm and enthusiasm for the new owner!' Fiona observed sarcastically.

Ian looked quickly at her and for the first time since her arrival, Fiona thought she saw a glint of humour in the dark grey eyes. If his next words had not been quite so dampening, she might have thought that their troubles would soon be a thing of the past.

'Aye, Sim'll be about average,' he said finally, clicking to his pony and leading the way across the yard. With her own mount following without any prompting, Fiona had nothing to do except absorb this daunting information and nothing more comforting to look at than Ian's rigidly straight back.

At first they rode in silence, single file up a narrow steep track, bare ploughed fields giving way to open moorland as they got further up. It stretched apparently limitlessly on either side of them and, apart from a few sheep cropping between the blackened heather roots, the moor was deserted. When they reached the top of the hill, the path widened into a small plateau and Ian turned in his saddle and beckoned Fiona up beside him.

'You can see most of the estate from up here,' he explained. 'Although you won't be able to tell where your land stops and your neighbour's begins. We don't go in for hedges and fences up here like you do down south. We use natural landmarks and cairns to mark our boundaries—like that cairn over there.'

He pointed to a cone-shaped pile of stones, about three feet high, just ahead of them.

'That marks the north-easternmost point of the

estate,' he went on in the easy rhythm of his deep, well-modulated voice. 'And this track here,' he waved to their left, 'runs around the northern boundary. It'll be about a fifteen-mile ride all told today to get around it. Are you game?'

'Of course!' Now that they were up here, all the minor pinpricks of the past twenty-four hours were as nothing compared to the dawning pride of ownership. Exhilarated by the wine-sharp air, Fiona felt she could have ridden five hundred miles that day if it had been demanded of her.

'Are you fit, then?' Ian was looking at her.

'Of course!' Fiona applied her heels to her pony's flanks and they set off again, riding side by side across the open moorland. Far below them on their left, the house stood like some fairytale castle in its hollow, its roofs and turrets shining in the sunlight.

'Most of the land up here is just left for rough pasture,' he explained as they jogged along, the ponies pacing effortlessly under their weight. 'We grow hay and cereals—oats and barley and so forth —in the fields below, but the rest is left for grazing and shooting.'

'Shooting?' Fiona was upset at the thought of shots shattering the peaceful stillness.

'Aye, a syndicate rents this stretch along here every year.'

'What do they shoot?' Fiona was already determined to put a stop to it.

'Oh, grouse and pheasant. We raise them in the

pens over there.' He pointed to a fenced copse of trees some way ahead.

'But that's terrible!' Fiona was even more horrified. 'You mean to say you raise the poor birds just to be shot?'

He looked across at her. 'You could say that,' he replied evenly, 'or you could say that we were increasing the productivity of land that would otherwise be barren—to say nothing of creating a food supply and employment.'

'Employment?' For the first of many times that day, Fiona did not understand.

'Aye, employment. Without the shoot Tom McPherson and his family would likely be on Welfare and your tenant farmers would have little enough left for the pleasures of life after they'd paid your rents.'

Fiona still did not understand.

'The McPhersons have been gamekeepers on this estate for generations,' Ian went on. 'Tom's the present one. Stop the shoot and you've no need for a gamekeeper, so unless Tom's prepared to move to the city, which I very much doubt, he'd be on the Welfare for most of the year, because there's little enough other work around here. As for the tenants, a few weeks' work every autumn as beaters means extra money for the men and lads—aye, and for some of the lassies, too.'

Fiona rode on in silence, absorbing this information. She was strongly against blood sports and had

refused to go fox-hunting ever since she had been
old enough to understand what it was all about, but
her new position as mistress of Craighill was obviously going to force her to re-think her attitude.
Had she the right to forbid the shoot when to do so
would severely affect the lives of those who had an
even greater right to look to her for support? She
had never expected her new life to be easy, but until
now she had not realised just how many difficult
decisions there would be.

Ian broke the silence, echoing her thoughts with
an uncanny accuracy.

'It's not easy, is it?' he asked. 'Reconciling inclination with responsibility? But if it weren't for
the shoot, you and I wouldn't be out riding on this
fine spring morning.'

'What do you mean?' Would the day ever come
when she would know everything about Craighill
without having to ask for an explanation? Fiona
wondered.

'Well, the ponies are kept for the shoot,' Ian explained. 'Most of the guns are businessmen, not used
to exercise and certainly not up to scrambling about
on the moors all day. We use the ponies to bring
them up from the house. There are a dozen or so,
all told.'

He could not have said anything more calculated
to distract her from the distasteful prospect of having to allow the pheasant shoot to continue, and she
looked about her at the empty moor.

'Where do you keep them?' she asked.

'Oh, they run free up here,' Ian said, 'but we'll likely see them during the day. Sim caught these two without too much trouble, so the rest are probably somewhere near the house.'

For once, he was wrong. The ponies were up on the high moorland.

They had stopped for lunch near the western cairn, unsaddling their own mounts to crop the short spring grass, and using the saddles as backrests while they ate the substantial lunch that Janet had prepared. At this height, with the surface water drained away into the valley below, the ground was warm and dry, and Fiona had been the first to see the group of dark shapes making their way tentatively towards them against the sun. She shaded her eyes and looked more closely.

'Are those the ponies?' she asked.

A few feet away from her, Ian raised himself on one elbow, squinting against the glare.

'Yes, that's them,' he said. 'Our two must have drifted away from the main herd.'

Attracted by the whickers of the riding ponies, the new arrivals came close enough for Fiona to be able to see them clearly. One or two appeared to be crossbreds, different in colour and size, but the rest were coal black with the sturdy bodies and short legs of the true Fell pony, known on the border between Scotland and England since Roman times as riding and pack animals.

Delighted with this unexpected bonus to her inheritance of Craighill, Fiona watched them graze. They were always on the alert for any sudden movement, but after a few minutes one of the mares moved aside, revealing a tiny foal standing there uncertainly on long spindly legs ending in neatly polished black patent hooves.

'Oh, look!' At the sound of Fiona's voice, the little fellow ran swiftly to his mother's flank and began nuzzling energetically.

'He's early,' Ian remarked. 'Born during the night, I should think. The foals don't usually come for another month at least. He probably couldn't wait to see the new owner!'

She was conscious of his giving her a sidelong glance from beneath his ridiculously long lashes and, absurdly, she found herself beginning to blush. She looked quickly back at the foal.

'I'll have to tell Sim to come up and take a look at him,' Ian said.

'Do you breed the ponies, then?' Although she could not resist the question, Fiona steadfastly kept her eyes on the animals in front of her.

'Not seriously, but we've got a stallion.' Ian paused, scanning the herd, and then he pointed. 'There! That tough-looking chap over there, do you see?'

Following the pointing finger, Fiona picked out an animal standing slightly apart, between them and the herd so that he could keep a watchful eye on both sides.

'The ponies were one of your great-uncle's hobbies, but for the past year or two he wasn't really up to taking much of an interest in them.'

'You must miss him a lot,' she said quietly.

'Yes, I do. We all do,' he went on after a pause. 'He was more than an employer to most of us.'

His expression more than his words brought the rumour that she had heard from the solicitor in London back to Fiona's mind. She studied him cautiously. It was true that he seemed more relaxed now that he was away from the great old house of Craighill with all its memories, but dared she ask him if he was really the old laird's son?

Curiosity was too strong. After all, she was entitled to know. If he was her great-uncle's natural son, they were related. Even so, she chose her words carefully.

'I'd heard that Sir Hector was your father.'

Ian looked across at her and for a second she thought she had gone too far. His face was taut with anger, and then he laughed without humour.

'So you've heard that old wives' tale, too, have you?' he said harshly. 'I suppose by now that I shouldn't be surprised, but I'm always amazed by how fast that particular piece of gossip travels!'

Chilled by the bitterness in his voice, Fiona spoke quickly. 'You've no need to tell me anything that you don't want to,' she said.

'No, that's all right. You have the right to know whether we're related. We're not! My own father did stay around long enough to marry my mother before he took off. My mother was a local girl and when my father took her to Glasgow and then deserted her, she came home. Your uncle took her in, made her his housekeeper and did more for me than my own father possibly could. He gave me a home, an education, looked after my mother and treated me like a son. The one thing he couldn't give me was his name, so I chose my mother's.'

Fiona would have liked to go on, to ask him what made him stay on at Craighill when everything that he had grown up to regard as his own had been passed into the hands of a stranger, but something about the set of his face stopped her. She had probed far enough.

So instead of talking she lay back, looking up into the clear blue sky and listening to the peaceful sounds of birdsong and of the ponies cropping the short grass. Her understanding silence was broken by Ian's voice, now much calmer.

'We'd better be making a move,' he said.

He got to his feet with the smooth, economical grace that was such a characteristic of all his movements and his shadow fell across her as he held out his hand. She took it. He pulled her up and they came suddenly face to face. Then Ian had turned away and was walking towards the ponies.

They caught their own two easily. The stallion

had moved the rest of the herd away · to a safe distance and Fiona could feel the bright intelligent eyes watching her as she saddled her mount. Their presence brought a sudden nostalgia for her own horse, Blue Fire.

'I've got a horse down in London,' she called across to Ian as she swung herself up into the saddle. 'I've been meaning to ask you about bringing her up here.'

'That should be no problem,' he replied. 'There's stabling enough in the yard, or else he can run on the moor with these fellows.'

'It's not a "he", it's a "she",' Fiona explained, pleased to be talking about Blue Fire again and wondering how she was doing. 'But she'll have to be kept indoors, I'm afraid—at least until the weather gets warmer.'

'In that case, Sim can fix a stall up for her in one of the barns,' Ian said. 'And there'll be plenty of good hunting up here for the pair of you next winter, if you're so inclined.'

'Oh, no, I'm not!' This time it was not the thought of killing live things as a sport that depressed Fiona. It was the prospect of winter itself.

She was not even sure that she would be able to stay at Craighill until then. By the time winter set in, she could well be back in London working for the educational television company that she had left when she had heard of her inheritance. Ian had inherited Sir Hector's fortune. The only income she could expect would be the rents from the tenant farmers, and these would certainly not be enough for her to live on far less to maintain Craighill. She would probably have to rent, if not sell completely, the solicitor had explained in London.

A million thoughts ran through her mind, but uppermost was the longing to be a part of Craighill. Now that she had seen it, had felt the pull of the land over which she was now riding, she longed with every fibre of her being to be a part of the way of life that had been fought for and preserved by generations of her ancestors, right down to her uncle, the old laird.

The man who was so much a part of that life, even though he had not been born a Montrose, broke into her thoughts.

'That's the Simpsons' place down there.' Ian had stopped and was pointing to a slate-roofed farmhouse just below them in the valley, protected from the worst of the wind and weather by a grove of fine trees.

'The Simpsons?' Fiona shaded her eyes against the sun high in the pale afternoon sky.

'Aye, one of your tenants. You know that there are four tenant farms as well as the house and the home farm, don't you?' Ian spoke slightly impatiently.

'Yes, I do, but I don't have to meet them today, do I?' Suddenly tired after everything that had happened not just in the last twenty-four hours but in the last few frantic weeks since she had heard about her inheritance, Fiona pleaded for time. Coming on top of everything else, the strain of meeting her tenants was more than she could face—particularly if they were going to be as unwelcoming as old Sim in the yard.

'You don't *have* to,' Ian replied, 'but they'll be eager to meet the new mistress.'

'As eager as old Sim?' Fiona said drily, and, to her relief Ian laughed.

'Aye,' he agreed, 'maybe you've got a point! And maybe you're right,' he went on after a pause, 'they still like the old ways up here. Maybe it would be better if we had a reception at the big house to introduce you properly. They'll not expect the new mistress to come dropping in unannounced in their back kitchens.' He made up his mind. 'No, a reception's the thing—I'll tell Macbeth to arrange it.'

Although he had called her the mistress of Craighill, that had not stopped him from taking things completely into his own hands again, Fiona realised. But her half real, half feigned resentment quickly began to fade as Ian started to talk.

He talked about the estate and the people on it with such a wealth of detail until she had no doubt why he had chosen to stay on at Craighill, rather than take the fortune that her great-uncle had left him and go elsewhere. He loved the place, every inch and stone and yard of it. Craighill was as much in his blood as it was in hers.

They turned for home and, far below them, Sim was a tiny figure pottering in the yard.

'Take old Sim now,' Ian went on. 'You'd never believe it to see him now but, at one time, old Sim was the smartest person around the place. That was when your uncle still hunted. Sim was his groom and off they would go together, every meet, fair weather or foul, your uncle in his old ratcatcher and Sim all polished and spruced up. A stranger would have been hard put to tell who was master and who was man! No one was closer to the old laird than Sim was in those days. . . .' His voice trailed away and the ponies' hooves on the springy turf became the only sound of the afternoon. 'Anyway,' he went on, 'there's one person who'll be pleased that you're bringing a horse with you to put in the old stables.' The grey eyes turned to her. 'Have you ridden long?'

'Since I was a child.' Fiona smiled into the eyes, forgetting all the earlier tensions and remembering only the pony that had always been waiting for her after school and during the holidays in the orchard at Hatchways, her Aunt Madeline's house in Kent. 'I was brought up by an aunt after my parents were killed in a car crash. Well, she's not my aunt, really. She was a cousin of my father's and much older than him. She's a funny old stick, but she had this feeling for horses—something like Sim and the old laird, I suppose.'

She slipped her tongue around the title by which

her great-uncle had been known. Its use pleased her, gave her a feeling of belonging, but then she looked quickly across at Ian, wondering if she had offended him. If she had, there was no outward sign of irritation on the handsome, set face, she noticed with relief.

'Will your aunt be joining you here?' he asked.

'Oh, no!' Fiona laughed at the thought of her comfort-loving Aunt Madeline in the rather austere surroundings of Craighill. 'She lives in Spain now. She suffers from arthritis and she sold her house in Kent last year because even Kent was too cold. I hardly think she'll be coming to Scotland.'

Once started, the story of how she had arrived on Madeline's doorstep at the age of seven, quite alone in the world since her parents' sudden death, came pouring out. It was the first time that she had really put into words the feelings of complete desolation that had struck her sixteen years before, when she had been told that her parents were dead and that she was to go and live with this unknown relative.

Until then, her life had been full of gaiety and love. Her father had been an actor, estranged from his family because of his determination to throw aside the legal career that had been planned for him and go on the stage. The estrangement had been complete when he had married an actress, and until she had seen the newspaper advertisement asking possible relatives of the late Sir Hector Montrose to contact a firm of London solicitors, Fiona had had only the vaguest idea that her father had been born in the Border country of Scotland.

She finished her story as they rode into the yard, realising that, unless she curbed her tongue, the man at her side would know as much about her as he obviously did about the lives of the estate tenants and workers. Even so, the thought did not displease her. Usually uneasy with strangers as she was, there was something as attractive about the personality of her companion as there was about the lean, muscular figure that housed it.

She shook herself and urged her pony on ahead. She was letting herself drift dangerously close to a fool's paradise. She could not possibly be attracted by a man she had known for less than twenty-four hours, particularly when that man had every reason to resent her existence. Ian Hamilton might be the estate manager, but she must never forget that he had grown up expecting to inherit Craighill, until she had appeared and seized it from him.

Sim was waiting for them and he took their ponies without a word, eyes going from one to the other of their smiling, relaxed faces, as though silently accusing them of disloyalty to the old laird's memory.

'Thank you, Sim.' Fiona made one last effort, but the retreating back stayed rigid with disapproval.

Once more, Ian surprised her. 'Don't worry,' he said, 'he'll come round. They'll all come round.'

As Ian himself would? Fiona wondered, looking up into the face above her. The next words spoke themselves. 'It's been a lovely day,' she said sincerely. 'I couldn't have asked for a better guide to introduce me to Craighill. Thank you so much, Mr Hamilton!'

'Ian.' The invitation for friendship that had been withheld earlier that morning was given in the one short word. And yet disappointment still lay in store. 'I'll be saying goodnight, then,' he went on.

'Goodnight? You're not coming indoors?' Her sense of anti-climax was so acute that it might have been physical.

'No—being away all day, I've got my final rounds to make.'

Fiona relaxed. 'So you'll be in for supper, then?' she said confidently.

'No, I'm afraid not.' His reply dashed her hopes once more. 'I'll be at the lodge this evening.'

'The lodge?' For the hundredth time that day, Fiona did not understand.

'Aye, the factor's lodge.'

'But if factor means what I think it means—which is estate manager—then aren't you the estate manager?'

'Yes, that's right.' Then he laughed, smacking his forehead with the palm of his hand. 'Macbeth's not told you, I'll be bound! She'll have blethered on about everything else, but the one thing she's obviously not told you is that when we heard you were coming, I moved out of the house into the lodge. It's over there.'

He waved a long-fingered hand in the direction of a grey slate roof just visible through the trees with a ragged wisp of smoke drifting up from its single chimney.

'But why did you move?' That first disappointment was as acute as all that was to follow in the weeks to come.

'Firstly, because it didn't seem right that I should stay in a house that now belongs to you,' Ian explained, 'and secondly because we didn't know what changes you might want to make—or who you might be bringing with you,' he added pointedly.

'But I've no one to bring with me!' Fiona replied a shade too fast and too eagerly for her own peace of mind. The last thing she wanted Ian to think was that she was giving him some sort of invitation by making it so clear that there was no special man in her life. 'I mean, I feel terrible about driving you out of your home,' she explained. 'Please say that you'll come back.'

Ian studied her. She imagined he was gauging her thoughts weighing up her meaning.

'No, I don't think so,' he said eventually. 'Having moved, I might just as well stay put.'

Then, with a brief 'Goodnight', he had turned on his heel and was walking away across the yard.

Remembering Bowser, Fiona made her own way towards the dog kennel, but disappointment stayed with her. It had been a perfect day and the crowning touch would have been to spend the evening talking it all over with the man who had made it possible.

The last thing she did that night before she went to bed was to draw the curtains of her room to make sure that the early morning light would wake her. Now that she knew it was there, she could just see the factor's lodge standing to one side of the big house, picked out in the moonlight. As she watched, the front door opened and two people came out and walked across the verge to the drive. One of them was Ian, but the smaller figure getting into the powerful-looking sports car parked outside and driving it expertly away was definitely that of a woman.

CHAPTER THREE

THE sun woke Fiona early the next morning. She got up eagerly and put on the blue trouser suit in which she had travelled to Scotland forty-eight hours earlier. She teamed it with a long-sleeved paisley blouse, tied at the neck in a soft bow to take away the slight touch of tailored severity and give her just the right look of femininity combined with competence that was suitable for the day ahead.

She had an appointment in Edinburgh with Kilgour and Scott, her great-uncle's solicitors. The legal firm she had dealt with in London had merely been acting as their agents and Fiona still had the formality of a meeting with Mr Kilgour to confirm her inheritance.

With a last tug at the edge of her jacket, she opened the bedroom door and made her way carefully down the steep flight of stairs to the kitchen. Bowser had been whining earlier on and she had put on her dressing gown and gone down and let him out into the yard. There was no sign of the dog now and Janet twitched her shoulders impatiently in the draught as Fiona stood in the open doorway calling him.

'He'll be away on business of his own!' the housekeeper said sharply. 'Come away in now and have your breakfast. There's no cause to worry yourself about that great beast—he can look after himself well enough.'

Fiona obediently closed the door and sat down. Ian's place at the table had already been cleared away, she noticed, although it was still barely eight o'clock. She would have to make her own early start to the day even earlier in future, she promised herself as she started on her porridge.

The sound of barking mixed with the urgent bleating came when she was half way through her meal. A man's shrill whistle cut through the noise, momentarily silencing it, but then the barking and the bleating began again. Already half suspecting what had happened, Fiona stood up and ran for the door, ignoring the housekeeper's protests.

The first thing she saw was a tightly bunched flock of sheep running in ever-decreasing circles of panic in the field at the back of the yard. Behind them, obviously having the time of his city-bred life, Bowser was barking madly. That was bad enough, but worse still was the sight of the tall figure of Ian Hamilton carefully taking aim along the double barrels of a lethal-looking shotgun. Fiona flew across the yard.

'No, don't!' she cried.

To her heightened senses, Ian's finger seemed to tighten fractionally on the trigger. Unthinking, she launched herself forward, trying to get past him and grab the gunbarrel and force it down. He shook her away with a ferocity that sent her sprawling backwards on to the ground and the gun went off with a deafening blast.

The echo of the shot died away and there was silence. No bleating, no barking, nothing except the harsh sound of two people breathing. Then the distant cawing of the rooks in the trees behind the house began to fill the still air with their clamour and Ian walked, white-faced, towards her.

'What the bloody hell do you think you're doing, woman?' His voice was thick with anger and with the relief that comes after sudden fear. 'I could have killed you!'

Lying on the gravel at his feet, Fiona realised that she had no defence. Her knowledge of guns was slight, but she knew that what she had attempted to do had been dangerously foolhardy. She struggled to stand on legs that were suddenly unwilling to bear her weight and Ian leaned forward, his fingers biting savagely into her arm as he pulled her roughly upright.

His face was only inches away and his breath was hot on her cheek. Suddenly, unaccountably, Fiona was trembling; trembling with an intensity that shook her very being. He released her and she stumbled. She fought for control, forcing herself to meet the blazing anger in his eyes.

'I want an explanation!' he demanded.

'I thought you were going to shoot Bowser,' Fiona

said lamely, noticing in spite of her confusion that the shotgun was now pointing safely downwards in the crook of his arm.

'Shoot the beast!' he echoed grimly. 'That's exactly what I will do if he worries my ewes again! But I'm hardly likely to do it while he's actually in the middle of the flock!'

'Then what were you going to do?' Fiona attempted to assert an authority as mistress of Craighill that she was far from feeling.

'Fire over his head and hope to scare the brute away!' Ian replied, his lips still thin and tight with anger. 'And in that, at least, it appears that I've succeeded.'

The sheep were still huddled in the corner of the field, but Bowser was coming towards them, the expression on his face that of a dog who considers his job well done. His happiness wavered as he got nearer and sensed the current of anger still flowing through Ian's rigid body. When he reached them, he dropped his tail and slunk nervously behind Fiona's legs for protection. Ian shot him a glance before turning his attention back to Fiona.

'If you remember, Miss Montrose,' he said with an icy formality, 'those are the yearling ewes I pointed out to you yesterday. Your ewes are always late in lambing, which is why I've had them brought down here. If, that is, we get any lambs at all after this morning's fiasco!'

'I'm sorry!' Fiona started to apologise, but his

voice cut across her like a whiplash.

'After yesterday, I would have thought that you would have had more sense! You're on a farm now —or had you forgotten?' he asked sarcastically. 'You may not value my advice, but if you value your livestock, perhaps you will consider taking it in future. From now on, keep that brute tied up. Good day, Miss Montrose!'

With one last angry glance, he had turned on his heel and strode off in the direction of the huddle of frightened sheep. Watching the grim, unyielding back it did not need his formal use of her name to tell Fiona that the mutual liking that had seemed to be springing up between them on their ride around the estate the previous day was already a thing of the past. She had entered his life unwanted and that was how he intended she should remain.

Bowser began to whine at her heels. Grabbing the offending dog by the collar, Fiona hauled him off in the direction of the kennel.

'And that's where you're going to stay, my lad!' she said, fixing the long chain to his collar. Then, touched by the bewildered expression in the melting brown eyes, she bent and patted the shaggy head. 'But you're new here, too, aren't you, old boy?' she said. 'And we've both obviously got a lot to learn!'

Fiona was still feeling shaky when she backed her car out of one of the barns to start her forty-mile journey to Edinburgh. Bowser was invisible in his kennel and she did not disturb him. Having between them antagonised Ian Hamilton to the point of no return, the last thing she wanted was to start the dog barking and upset Janet as well.

Melrose was the first stage on her journey and once she had negotiated the little Border town, the roads were empty and the drive through the beautiful Border countryside began to calm her. Everywhere was beginning to show the first faint hints of a northern spring and Fiona drove slowly, looking out at the bare ploughed fields and open moorland rolling away on either side of her. It did not take long before she realised that she was looking at it with a new eye. Where once she would have been entirely absorbed with its beauty, now she was thinking about its potential crop and stock yield, trying to remember everything that her guide had taught her the day before.

The thought of Craighill's estate manager brought a rush of regret. Yesterday they had seemed to be on the verge of friendship—now they were almost enemies. She could even forgive him his intolerably high-handed behaviour over Bowser that morning. After all, she had been entirely in the wrong. If only she had taken his advice and kept the dog tied up, the dawning liking that had seemed to be growing between them on their ride together might not have been destroyed.

And yet had that morning's incident really made

any difference? Had the gulf between them ever really lessened? Even yesterday, Fiona recalled, it had only been when they had been on the open moorland talking about Craighill that the air of reserve with which Ian had treated her had been temporarily lifted and dispersed. He had also left her abruptly as soon as they got back to the house. What more did she need to tell her that it was Craighill that he valued; it was certainly not her friendship or her desire to please.

From that moment, she drove hard, pushing the car and concentrating on the road, but even so she was late for her appointment. Two-thirty had been the time stipulated in the letter that she had received from Kilgour and Scott and it was already well past that before she had even managed to find a parking space. For some reason, the Scottish capital of Edinburgh was particularly crowded on that bright spring day. The first of April, Fiona suddenly realised. All Fools' Day—and what a fool she had already been!

When at last she reached the solicitors' offices she was flushed and breathless.

'Good afternoon!' The young girl sitting behind the desk did not have one blonde hair out of place and she took in Fiona's dishevelled appearance at a disapproving glance.

'Oh, good afternoon.' Feeling her disadvantage, Fiona spoke uncertainly. 'I have an appointment with Mr Kilgour.'

A faint line of query appeared between the finely plucked brows as if the girl was doubting that such an obviously inferior person could possibly have business with one of Edinburgh's leading solicitors.

'And who shall I say is calling?' The refinement of her true Edinburgh accent made every syllable precise.

'Oh—er—Fiona Montrose.'

'Please be seated, Miss Montrose.' The girl got up and disappeared through the door behind her, leaving Fiona to find a chair and surreptitiously comb her hair.

'Mr Kilgour will see you straight away.' The elegant blonde had returned and the look that caught Fiona's comb disappearing back into her bag was even more disapproving. Completely crushed, Fiona followed her through into the inner office. If Mr Kilgour's secretary was like this, what on earth would the lawyer himself be like? she wondered.

'Good afternoon, Miss Montrose.' The pouches underneath Alexander Kilgour's elderly eyes gave him a look of almost Oriental inscrutability and Fiona could not tell how irritated or otherwise he might be at her late arrival. His handshake was cool and impersonal and his voice, with that same clipped Edinburgh accent, gave nothing away.

'Will that be all, Mr Kilgour?' The secretary, standing in the doorway, cut sharply across their greeting.

'Yes, Miss ... um ...' He fumbled for the name

and then looked sheepishly away. 'A temporary girl,'
he explained when the door had closed behind her.
'But only until my Miss Diamond gets back!' he
added more happily.

Fiona relaxed. The little incident had made him
more human and she could even imagine a hint of
curiosity in the guarded legal eyes about the young
woman who had appeared so unexpectedly to claim
his late client's estate. A hint of curiosity that was
confirmed the moment they were seated facing each
other across the broad leather-topped desk.

'First, I must congratulate you,' the solicitor began. 'You are indeed a very fortunate young woman,
and I believe the bequest came as a considerable surprise?'

Fiona risked a smile. 'It did indeed,' she said. 'Until I answered the advertisement, I knew nothing
about my great-uncle or even about my grandfather.
Aunt Madeline. . . .'

'Aunt Madeline?' Mr Kilgour interrupted ques-
tioningly.

'Yes, a distant cousin of my father's,' Fiona explained. 'She brought me up when my parents were
killed. At the time, there was no one else.'

'I see. And you, of course, are the daughter of
James Montrose?'

'That's right.' Fiona noticed that the papers on
the desk were those that she had already signed in
London.

'Had your father not died, he would have inherited Sir Hector's title as well as the estate,' the solicitor said. 'But even in this day and age'——he allowed himself a slight smile—'a woman may not inherit the baronetcy of Craighill. It's a pity—a pity that it should die out. And what, if I may ask, are your plans for the estate, Miss Montrose?' he went on after a pause.

'My plans?' Fiona was a little surprised at the question. 'Well, I shall keep it, of course, and I hope I shall be able to live there.'

'But, my dear girl!' The solicitor looked amazed. 'Surely it has been explained to you that there is no income at all with your inheritance? True, there are the rents from the tenant farm, but they are not large, and they—and more besides—will be needed for the upkeep of the home farm and the house itself. If Sir Hector's personal fortune had not been left elsewhere, then it might have been a different matter. But as it is,' he shrugged his shoulders in gentle sympathy, 'you have no choice but to sell.'

'You're quite sure there's no other way?' This was what the solicitor in London had hinted at, but Fiona felt even more miserable now that her worst fears were confirmed.

Touched by her evident distress, the solicitor paused and thought more carefully.

'It had never occurred to me that a young woman coming from London would want to keep Craighill,' he admitted, 'but perhaps there is a way. Perhaps it could be leased. The estate as a whole is potentially very profitable, but after the inroads of death duties, it needs the resources of considerable capital behind it, and that capital, of course, has gone to Mr Hamilton.'

Fiona sat, only half comprehending, while Mr Kilgour went on to explain the intricacies of capital gains tax, amortisation, liquidity and replenishment of stock. He seemed to be explaining as much to refresh his own mind as for Fiona's benefit, but at the end of it all, he still advised her to sell. The one thing she could not afford to do was to keep Craighill.

Fiona's whole being rebelled against the prospect. Even in the short time that she had been there, Craighill had become her roots. Roots that had twice been taken from her: once when her parents had been killed and then again, the previous year, when Aunt Madeline had gone to Spain. Hatchways, the house in which she had grown up, had been sold, and Fiona had been left to live alone in London.

Finally, she was out of the solicitor's office with her decision still to be made. The drive from Edinburgh that had touched her with its beauty that morning now became a mechanical chore to be accomplished as quickly as possible. Every passing field and stretch of moorland only served to emphasise the inescapable fact that Craighill could not be hers.

By the time she had reached Melrose, the beautiful day had turned into an even more beautiful pink twilight. The Eildon Hills and the distant line of the Cheviots were spread out in front of her under a spectacular sky of violet and gold, but Fiona was oblivious to the beauty of it all. Her head was full of a thousand thoughts. Her mind was spinning and yet her brain was numb. When she turned in between the tall stone gateposts of Craighill, she was no nearer a decision than she had been when she had left Edinburgh.

She longed to talk things over, but who was there to turn to? Aunt Madeline was in Spain and she had lost touch with all her university friends. Even though she had only met him twice, the thought that Geoff Gilson might have been an ideal choice suddenly struck her. But Geoff was away in Africa building bridges—and there was no one.

No, not quite! There was Ian. The more Fiona thought about it, the less fantastic the idea became. He had shown that morning that he had very little time for her personally and if it had not been for her, he would have inherited the estate as well as the substantial fortune that her great-uncle had left him, but on the other hand, his feelings about Craighill were just as strong as her own. He would be affected just as much as everyone else on the estate if she had to sell. Whatever he might think about her personally, surely he could not refuse to discuss the future of Craighill.

Fiona parked her car outside the factor's lodge. There were no lights in the windows, but a thin plume of smoke was coming from the chimney and a Land Rover was parked outside. Ian was probably there. Making up her mind, Fiona got out of the car and walked up to the front door.

Ian answered the door quickly and for a second she had the uncanny feeling that he had been expecting her. She looked up, scanning the dark face for any sign of anger.

'I wondered if I could have a word with you,' she said hesitantly.

'Surely!' His tone was easy. 'Come in.'

Fleetingly conscious of his closeness, Fiona stepped across the threshold into the pungent smell of woodsmoke. The door led straight into the living room and the room was dark, lit only by the burning log fire. Heavy beams brought the ceiling down almost to the level of Ian's head and the furniture was ugly and old-fashioned. The only touch of colour was a pink scarf, flung carelessly down on to the coffee table in front of the hearth. It lay there, like a brightly coloured bird arrested in mid-flight, all the time they talked.

'Sit down.' Ian pointed to one of the over-stuffed armchairs by the fire. 'It's not really what you would call a home from home, I'm afraid, but it serves its purpose. A girl from one of the farms comes in every morning to clean and she'll leave a meal for me if I want it. Would you like a drink?'

'No, no, thank you.' She had quite enough on her mind without alcohol, Fiona thought, watching Ian lower his lean body into the chair facing her and struggling to draw at least the tattered remnants of her authority as mistress of Craighill around her as some protection against his quizzical stare.

'What can I do for you?' he asked eventually.

She took the plunge. 'I've come for your advice, as a matter of fact,' she said.

He laughed. 'My advice?' he queried, one dark eyebrow lifting ironically. 'I should have thought that my advice would have been the last thing you would be interested in!'

Fiona remembered. 'I'm sorry about this morning, I really am!' she said desperately. 'I know I should have done what you told me and kept Bowser tied up. He will be from now on. How are the sheep?'

'As it happens, they're fine,' he said. 'No harm done. Maybe I was a mite over-hasty.' He paused, letting Fiona absorb the nearest thing to an apology that she had heard from him. 'Now, what can I do for you?'

'It looks as though I've got to sell Craighill. I can't afford to keep it and as you, as well as everyone else on the estate, will be affected whatever I do, I thought I would like to discuss it with you before I came to any decision.'

Fiona heard herself gathering speed as she went on. At the end of her little speech she stopped, slightly breathless, expecting shock, amazement, alarm, anything except the tone of calm assurance with which her estate manager eventually replied.

'I was wondering when it would come to this,' he said.

'You were wondering? But how could you? I don't understand,' Fiona blurted out.

'You're forgetting that I'm your co-heir,' Ian explained, 'and also that it took a long time to find you after the old laird died. In fact, at one stage it seemed as if I was going to inherit in default of any blood relative appearing on the scene. So the financial situation isn't really news to me.'

'Oh, I see!' Fiona breathed, everything suddenly falling into place. As heir to her great-uncle's fortune, of course Ian had also been to see Mr Kilgour.

She waited for him to go on, but he remained silent, forcing her to take the initiative.

'Then what do you suggest?' she asked finally. 'You must have thought about it.'

'Indeed I have,' he replied seriously. 'And I've thought about it even more since you came here. My suggestion is that we get married.'

In the silence that followed, the ticking of the clock seemed unnaturally loud: each second marking off what seemed to be eternity.

'I'm quite serious,' Ian said at last. 'Looked at from the point of view of a business proposition, it's the sensible thing to do. Even with the old laird's money, I can't afford to buy you out, and you can't afford to run the estate. But once married, we should own everything jointly and everything could continue as before.'

Except for the small point that she would then have a husband and he a wife, Fiona thought.

'It's not such a wild idea as it seems,' he went on. 'Craighill has been my life and I would fight to preserve every inch of it. In a different way, it's in my blood just as much as it's in yours—and you feel that already, don't you? I've seen it in your face.'

The feeling of pride mixed with responsibility that had grown inside her during their long ride together around the boundaries of the estate returned to stir Fiona deeply. She nodded.

'Then in that case, we have no choice.' Ian spoke quickly and confidently as though there could be as little doubt in Fiona's mind as in his own. 'We must marry. Together we can save Craighill—put it back on a good financial footing. When that's done, we may have to think again, but for now marriage is the obvious solution. Unless, that is, there's already somebody else?'

He glanced at her, an unfathomable look in his eyes.

'No, there's no one else.' Fiona brushed aside the fantastic notion that he might really be concerned about a rival for her affections, and studied the man who had just asked her to sacrifice her future for the sake of Craighill.

It was certainly not the first time that a marriage had been arranged to preserve an estate along the

Border. Maybe it had even been done before to save Craighill, but at the end of the twentieth century it was unbelievable. A sense of unreality overtook her. In the flickering firelight, the figure facing her, tense and expectant like a finely coiled spring, could well be some ancient Border laird about to sweep his bride away to her marriage bed. The dark hawklike features and the strong muscular body sent an involuntary tremor running through her at the thought of surrendering to the demands he would then have the right to make.

She checked herself firmly. What was being proposed was not a marriage from which she could expect love and children but a marriage of convenience to save the land that they both loved from falling into the hands of strangers. She could be under no illusions about that. He had no need to explain.

Lost in thought, she stared into the twisting flames, not hearing Ian get to his feet and move impatiently to her side. The touch of his hand on her shoulder startled her and she drew back slightly, as if hoping to find refuge in the recesses of the big wing chair and delay the moment when her decision would have to be made. Her movement made his hand rest more heavily.

'Have you decided?' he asked. His voice was low, but Fiona barely heard it through the pounding of her heart as his fingers moved first from her shoulder to the whiteness of her throat and then up its length to cup her chin with a cool hand that had the touch of fire.

In spite of herself, she moved towards him, shifting her weight imperceptibly in the chair, driven by such a strong urge to touch him that she was afraid—afraid of herself and of the sensations that were sweeping through her, sensations based on a need that she had never known before.

How could she marry him on the basis of a business arrangement when she knew now, and for all time, that he was the man she loved?

'I must have more time to think,' she said.

'There is no time,' Ian replied. 'The future of Craighill must be settled—now. If words won't convince you, perhaps this will!'

Before she could protest, he had drawn her from her chair, holding her close against him, locked in the encircling strength of his arms as his lips came down to claim her, and everything was lost in the sensation of liquid fire running through her veins.

After the first moment of complete surprise Fiona forced herself to resist, putting her hands against his shoulders and rigidly denying the searching pressure of his mouth as it made every fibre of her being come alive.

It was a trick, she told herself desperately. This wasn't love. It was Craighill he wanted, not her. He could not have made it more clear that he was interested in her as a business partner, nothing more. She had taken the estate from him and now all he wanted was to preserve the inheritance that he had grown up expecting to be his until the day when he could buy her out and reclaim his own.

This kiss was just a calculated ruse to force her heart to rule her head and force her to agree. But she would not give in. She would not surrender to the sudden, stirring passion rising inside her. She would marry him, she knew that now, but she would make it clear that her acceptance was on the basis of his proposal. It would be a marriage of convenience to save Craighill. He would never know how much she longed for something more.

With a furious strength, she broke away and Ian stood back, looking down at her with fathomless grey eyes, a smile twisting his narrow mouth in what could have been self-mockery.

'And now that you have made it absolutely clear that I hold no attraction for you at all,' he said, 'will you give me your reply? Are you prepared to sacrifice yourself for the sake of the estate?'

'Yes,' Fiona said through trembling lips. 'I'll marry you to save Craighill, but as a business arrangement, nothing more.'

CHAPTER FOUR

THEY agreed before they parted that their marriage should be kept a secret. Ian would stay on in the factor's lodge and Fiona would continue to live alone in the big house. Mr Kilgour would be asked to draw up an agreement and make arrangements for a quiet civil ceremony in Edinburgh, and he was to be the only person to know the truth.

But it was not such an easy matter to keep the plan a secret from Janet. The housekeeper's devotion to Ian was becoming increasingly apparent, and along with that devotion was a thinly disguised scheme of her own to provide a solution to the problems at Craighill.

After her acceptance of Ian's incredible proposal, Fiona had had a disturbed and almost sleepless night, but Janet was not to be denied her moment of glory of showing the new mistress around the house. Unwilling to disappoint her, Fiona had given in and she found herself following in the tiny housekeeper's footsteps the next morning as they went from room to room.

'The old place used to be full of life in the old days, so I've been told,' said Janet, her voice echoing off the high walls and ceilings. 'But that was when the old laird was young—before my time and before the young master's time, too!'

'Have you been here long, Janet?' Fiona asked, defeated in her attempts to people the empty corridors and huge rooms with the ghosts of the happy, laughing young people she had seen in the faded photographs in her uncle's room. All that cried out to her from the echoing spaces and the dusty sheet-covered furniture was the emptiness of her great-uncle's later life and the lonely frustration of his death.

'Aye, I've been here quite a while,' said Janet. 'I came to Sir Hector when my old mother died—that would be ten years ago when the young master was still away at agricultural college. I never thought I'd stay. Coming from Glasgow to a great empty barn of a place like this with just myself and the old laird to live here. The only time there was any life was when young Master Ian came home for the holidays. Every time he went back, I told myself that I'd be leaving, too, but then the next holidays would be coming and I'd stay a while longer!'

'And now Mr Hamilton's here all the time,' Fiona remarked.

'Aye, and that's more to the good!' Janet said fondly before going back to her memories. 'A great skinny lad he was in those days, though. Not that that bothered the lassies! They were round the house like bees round a jam pot the moment the young master came home. A great one for the lassies, he was in the old days!'

'And what about now?' Fiona remembered the woman in the sports car that she had seen leaving the factor's lodge the night after her arrival. Was her husband-to-be still 'a great one for the lassies'? she wondered.

'Lord bless you, no! And that's more the pity!' Janet replied. 'Until yourself, there's not been a lassie in the house since the old laird died. The young master took it hard, and a great house like this needs a bit of young life, to say nothing of a few bairns to liven it up.' Having made her point, she shot Fiona a speculative glance. 'There's a great set of nurseries on the upper floor,' she went on innocently. 'Will you be wanting to see them?'

Did she? She might as well, Fiona thought. Even though she and Ian would never have the children to fill them, there would be no harm in going and looking at the rooms in which generations of her ancestors had grown up.

Janet went on ahead up yet another flight of narrow stairs. Fiona wondered what her reaction would be if the housekeeper knew that the marriage she so obviously had in mind had already been arranged, but her speculations stopped abruptly the moment they reached the upstairs landing. No children of hers would ever grow up in the nurseries of Craighill, Fiona vowed.

The rooms that opened out on either side of the dingy passageway were more like a prison than a nursery. Small, with low ceilings and barred windows, they were places where children were expected to grow up both unseen and unheard. A creaking service lift that came up from the kitchen even made it unnecessary for them to go downstairs for meals.

The only time they emerged, Fiona supposed, was when, neatly dressed and on their best behaviour, they were taken downstairs for a daily meeting with their parents. No wonder her grandfather and her great-uncle had died lonely and estranged old men if their childhood had been as austere and unloving as these rooms proclaimed. She shivered. She might have committed herself to a loveless marriage, but no child deserved a similar upbringing.

Yet how stupid to be thinking of children when the agreement she had made the night before with Ian ensured that there would be none in her life for years to come!

Fiona was still brooding on the prospect when she sat across the supper table from Ian that night. She was so absorbed that she jumped at the noise when Janet set the coffee pot down in front of her.

'I'll be away to turn down your bed, then,' Janet said.

'What?' Startled out of her thoughts, Fiona half rose from her chair. 'There's no need to do that,' she said.

'I always did it for the old laird,' Janet replied firmly, 'and I daresay the two of you will have enough to talk about without me being here!' she added pointedly, walking briskly to the door and shutting it behind her.

'Would you say the good Janet might have some ulterior motive in leaving us alone together?' Ian's smile was dry.

It was the first time they had been alone together since his proposal; since she had torn herself away from the embrace that had been calculated to make her agree. Fiona checked herself, forcing herself to remember that, like his first kiss, his smile now was aimed at only one end; to ensure that she go through with their marriage to save Craighill. Now was the time to make it clear that she understood.

'Then Janet's going to be disappointed, isn't she?' Frustrated anger and emotion gave her voice an edge. 'We both know that what we're planning is purely a business arrangement and that if there was any alternative, neither of us would ever consider it.'

The expression on his face was inscrutable. 'In that case,' he said, 'you'll be pleased to hear that I've made an appointment for us both to go and see Kilgour tomorrow to have the legal documents properly drawn up.'

'Good!' Fiona stood up with a harsh scraping of her chair. 'And now, if you'll excuse me, as you've made the appointment, I think I ought to go and study the papers in my room to make sure that I'm properly prepared.'

Minutes later, as she sat at her great-uncle's desk

in the room that had also been his, it was not the old laird's face but Ian's that kept coming between Fiona's eyes and the documents that she was desperately trying to study. Had it not been so incredible, she would have said that she was already half in love with the man who had asked her to be his wife. But the thought was as impossible as the notion that she would ever give up Craighill while there was the slightest chance of saving it.

It seemed only fitting that the rain should be pouring down out of a leaden April sky when the formal signing of the legal papers detailing the joint ownership of the estate and the substantial fortune that now went with it finally took place in the solicitor's Edinburgh office. The agreement was not to come into force until the day of their marriage and, after the signing, Mr Kilgour asked for a few moments alone with Fiona.

'Miss Montrose, are you certain that you are fully cognisant of what you are doing?' The precise voice coming across the desk had the definite edge of disapproval.

'Yes, I think so,' said Fiona.

'With all due respect,' the voice grew more acid, 'I would suggest that you should be more certain than merely "thinking". The consequences of the step that you are about to take will undoubtedly affect your whole life. How it will do this, only time will tell, but, as the owner of Craighill, you are contributing by far the greater part of the marriage settlement. The late Sir Hector's fortune was sizeable but by no means comparable to the value of the estate. It is no exaggeration to say that you would be a very wealthy woman if you were to sell and, as such, the possessor of considerable freedom.'

How could she explain that she did not want freedom? Fiona thought. Her need to stay on at Craighill had grown stronger, not weaker, in the two weeks that had elapsed since she had sat in that same chair and listened to Ian outlining their plans for saving the estate to the highly disapproving solicitor's ears. And although she had struggled to deny it, it was no longer just her need for roots that drove her on. The love that had lain dormant in her heart ever since her parents' death had been irresistibly awakened by the man whose signature now stood beside hers on the legal documents in front of her.

It was an impossible love, one that she could never acknowledge, but she could not give it up while there was the slightest chance that it might one day be returned.

Mistaking the quiet desperation in Fiona's face for obstinacy, Mr Kilgour allowed himself a silent comment on the wrong-headedness of modern youth and slipped the documents into a leather folder. There was clearly no point in attempting further persuasion.

'Then if your mind is quite made up,' he said, pressing the buzzer on his desk, 'all I can do is to ensure that you have the utmost protection the law allows. Come in!'

He raised his voice in answer to the brief tap on the door and managed a wintry smile for the plump secretary who had returned to take the place of the supercilious young girl Fiona had encountered on her first visit to his office.

'Ah, Miss Diamond,' he said. 'Kindly tell Mr Hamilton that Miss Montrose and I have finished our business and that he may come in.'

Ian did not ask what Mr Kilgour had said and they made the drive home in the constrained silence that had been growing between them over the past few days. Although he was now her fiancé and this was a time when there should have been great intimacy between them, he seemed even more distant— as if to underline the purely business nature of their agreement.

Tradition demanded that he be at her side the next afternoon, every inch her estate manager, when the presentation of the tenants to the new mistress of Craighill took place. Although she had been dreading it, Fiona had been able to put off the occasion no longer and she had had the big reception room at the front of the house opened up for the occasion.

The dust-sheets covering the furniture had been removed and a fire had been lit in the ornate marble fireplace, but its warmth did little to dispel the chilly atmosphere as the line of tenants and employees passed by, making little or no attempt to respond to Fiona's efforts at friendship. Most of them probably thought that the man by her side had been unfairly treated by the conditions of the old laird's will, she thought, as she shook hand after hand and looked into eyes expressing various degrees of resentment. To the heirs of generations of Border warfare, Scots against English, it must be bad enough that she had come from England, but to them she was also a usurper, plucked out of nowhere to take the place that rightfully belonged to the 'young master'.

No matter how many assurances she gave that their lands and their jobs were safe and that nothing would be changed at Craighill, the faces remained dour and suspicious. By the time the last tenant had left, Fiona had reached screaming pitch at the futility of trying to make a favourable impression on this wall of human hostility.

But worse, far worse, than the tenants' reception was the appearance of the low-slung sports car outside the factor's lodge every night. In spite of Janet's belief to the contrary, its presence was proof that Fiona was not the only woman in her future husband's life and she found herself listening for it to leave before she could drop off into an uneasy sleep. For the first time, she knew what it was to be jealous and she hated herself, Ian and, above all, the unknown woman for whom he left her after supper every night.

The one happy occasion during the time that it was to take Mr Kilgour to finalise the arrangements for their marriage should have been the arrival of

Blue Fire, but even that was marred.

The horse had come by train to Glasgow and had then been boxed to Craighill. Fiona heard the heavy scrunch of wheels on gravel late one afternoon and hurried out into the yard. She could hear Blue Fire kicking impatiently against the partition in the horsebox even before the loading ramp was down, and when the driver led her out she was jumpy and her dapple grey shoulders were flecked with sweat. Seeing Fiona, she half reared and plunged towards her, almost dragging the rope from the driver's hand.

'That's all right!' Fiona called to the startled man. 'Let her go—she'll be all right!'

Only too pleased, the man threw the halter rope around the mare's neck. For a moment she stood there, pawing the ground and snorting uncertainly. Then, lowering her head, she charged full gallop across the space separating them and slid to a halt only inches away, nuzzling for the sugar that Fiona generally had in her pocket.

'Here you are, girl!' Fiona held out the expected offering and Blue Fire took it with delicately out-stretched lips. The sugar disappeared and she stood snorting gently through flared nostrils.

'*That* was quite an entrance!'

A familiar voice came quietly from behind Fiona's shoulder, surprising them both. The mare reared, neighing her alarm, iron-shod hooves thrash-ing the air dangerously close to their heads. Fiona stepped back instinctively and found herself against the hard strength of Ian's body. She felt his arm go protectively around her.

'Steady! Steady, horse!' Ian's voice was low, calm, without fear of the sudden crushing death hovering only fractionally above them as the mare reared and reared again.

'Be still!' The note of authority finally penetrated the animal's primitive panic and she responded, to stand trembling but quiet in front of them.

Releasing his hold on Fiona, Ian moved forward to take the halter, crooning to the still quivering animal with a gentleness that Fiona had not suspected he possessed.

'And that,' he said, when Blue Fire was finally calm, continuing their conversation as if they had not been interrupted by the wildly thrashing hooves, 'is quite an animal! I forget sometimes that all horses aren't quite as placid as the fellows we keep out on the moor. What do you intend to do with her? She's too fine a beast just to keep for country rides.'

Fiona's body was still tingling with the aftermath of fear and with the shock of Ian's closeness when she had stumbled back into his arms, and she paused for a moment before she replied.

'I'm hoping that she'll make a good three-day event horse,' she said eventually.

Ian ran a hand down the mare's shoulder and for a second it seemed all constraint between them had vanished and they could have been back on the open moorland on the day of their first happy ride together.

Then he spoke and the illusion was shattered.

'In that case,' he said casually, 'you must have a word with Isobel Carstairs. She's a walking diary for the social events around here, and I think she said something last night about a three-day event at Peebles on the twenty-eighth.'

A cold icy anger flooded through Fiona. Not only had Ian confirmed her suspicions about the driver of the sports car parked outside his cottage night after night but, with their own wedding just days away, he did not even consider it necessary to hide the fact that he was continuing a liaison with another woman.

He could not have made it more clear that he regarded their marriage as completely and utterly one of convenience. What a fool she had been to think that the love that was even now betraying her as she looked at the tall figure standing by the horse's side could ever be returned. He was not interested in love. His only interest was in Craighill!

Trembling with emotion, Fiona snatched the halter rope out of his hand and blurted out the first words that came into her head.

'A three-day event isn't a social occasion,' she said cuttingly. 'It's a horse trial!'

She could sense him looking after her, as she walked off across the yard with Blue Fire following obediently at her heels.

By the time the sun came up, red and angry, the following morning, Fiona made up her mind to call the marriage off. She could not endure the constant humiliation, the never-ending sleepless nights.

She felt tired, hot gravel behind her eyes, but she groomed Blue Fire as though her life depended on it. Mr Kilgour had been right. She was on the verge of ruining her life for an impossible dream. Nothing, not even the security of Craighill, was worth the misery of loving and knowing that her love could never be returned.

There was no alternative: she would sell the estate. Provisos could be written into the sale guaranteeing the jobs and livelihoods of those dependent on it for support, and she would go back to London. Even if such safeguards decreased the value of the property, they would at least salve her conscience and she would still be rich. Rich and free to go anywhere in the world. The only thing that was wrong with her plan, she suddenly realised, was that there was nowhere in the world she wanted to be except Craighill. At Craighill with Ian Hamilton at her side; her husband in the fullest and truest sense of the word.

Cramped after her long journey, Blue Fire joyously climbed the steep track that Fiona had ridden with Ian such a lifetime of experience and heartache before. The mare's pace was quicker than that of the sturdy fell ponies and they soon reached the stone cairn that marked the northernmost boundary of the estate. Balancing herself in the saddle, Fiona let the willing horse out into a long steady gallop across the moorland top.

The spinney in which the pheasants were raised came rushing towards them as they moved effortlessly through the still morning air: girl and horse at one with each other and with their surroundings. The man who came walking slowly round the corner of the little wood stood watching appreciatively as they thundered towards him.

It was the gamekeeper, Tom McPherson. Fiona pulled the mare up and smiled down at him. Tom had been the only person to show even the slightest hint of response to her efforts at friendship during that never-ending afternoon when she had met the tenants. Like most of the people on the estate, Tom was small; not more than five foot five, Fiona guessed. His resemblance to old Sim, the yard man on the home farm, was so strong that they might have been brothers, but the resemblance ended sharply when it came to their eyes. Sim's eyes were dark and spacious, peering out from under shaggy brows like some furry hedge animal sensing danger, but Tom's held a friendly alertness, his smile reaching to their corners and crinkling the weatherbeaten skin into a network of tiny lines.

'Good morning!' From her vantage point on Blue Fire's back, Fiona smiled down at the gamekeeper.

'Aye, it's a braw one at that!' came the steady reply. 'And that's a fine animal you've got there, Miss Montrose.'

'Yes, she is, isn't she?' Fiona's voice softened with the pride of ownership. 'She came up from London yesterday.'

'Then she'll be pleased to be here.' Tom spoke as though there could be no doubt as to any creature's preference for the Borders over London. Stepping forward, he patted the mare approvingly on the neck. Blue Fire snorted and backed away.

'What's wrong, girl?' Fiona tightened her grip on the reins, wondering what was upsetting the mare. Surely not this slow countryman with his obvious way with animals?

'Och, it'll be the blood,' Tom said apologetically.

'The what?'

'The blood.' He held out his hand and a very large and very dead weasel unfolded itself to swing slowly by its tail.

Blue Fire snorted again.

'Ugh! What are you going to do with that?' Fiona asked distastefully.

'Nail it to my gibbet,' Tom replied matter-of-factly. 'It's down there a wee way.'

He pointed a gnarled finger and Fiona could just make out what might have been a row of small corpses nailed to the spinney fence.

'Some folks say it's nothing but superstition,' he went on, 'but spike one of these laddies to the fence and the rest will stay away. Aye, and it's the same

with the rats and with the old crow and with anything else that'll fancy a pheasant chick or an egg for
itself!'

Take a life to preserve life, Fiona thought, reminded of the pattern of conservation that Ian had
explained to her on their ride together. The thought
of Ian brought another in its wake and now seemed
as good a time as any to seek an answer.

'Tom,' she asked, 'why don't the others seem to
like me? The tenants, I mean. You're friendly
enough, but the rest look at me as if I was some
monster from outer space!'

'Aye, well, you come from England,' he said, as if
that explained a lot. 'And you're a lassie, too. They
don't care to see a lassie in a man's place.'

So much for Women's Lib. north of the Border,
Fiona thought, amused in spite of herself, but Tom
was going on and she listened carefully.

'They're set in the old ways,' he said, 'with the old
laird and the young master. They wouldna' care to
see him put out.'

'And you?' Fiona asked, surprised at how suddenly important his answer was. 'Do you care, too,
Tom?'

'Aye, I care,' he said evenly, meeting her blue
eyes with his brown ones. 'But you're a Montrose
for all that and the Montroses have always looked
after their own. You may have had the misfortune
to be born in that other place——' he shrugged a
shoulder dismissively southwards, 'and you may be

a lassie, but you canna deny your blood!'

Walking Blue Fire down the last quarter of a mile back to the house to cool her down, Fiona turned the gamekeeper's words over in her mind for the hundredth time. It did not take much imagination to realise that Tom had been speaking for everyone on the estate when he had spoken about the responsibility that she had inherited along with Craighill. The tenants, the workers, their families, Ian, Janet and Tom himself— she would be altering their lives irrevocably if she sold. No one individual would be able to afford to buy an estate of that size and if she sold it would have to be to a business consortium; maybe even to a consortium from one of the oil-rich Arab countries that had recently begun to invest in Britain. Whatever safeguards were written into the sale, what possible concern could she fairly expect an investment group to have in the welfare of the individual?

She looked down at the house, roofs and turrets shining in the moody April sunshine. A huge white elephant better torn down for its land value than kept standing. Twisting in the saddle, she looked back at the hills, fought over and preserved by generations of Montroses. Then, finally and sightlessly, she looked into the future from which there was no escape. Marriage to a man who did not love her, in order to preserve Craighill.

CHAPTER FIVE

'HAPPY the bride the sun shines on.' The saying could not have been more inappropriate, Fiona thought, glancing at the expressions on the faces around her. It was her wedding day and the sun was indeed shining, streaming in through the stained glass windows and turning the greens, golds and blues in the coat of arms of the City of Edinburgh into a distorted pattern on the marble floor of the registrar's outer office.

Ian was pacing restlessly up and down and the sight of his tall, lean figure, accentuated by the finely cut dark worsted of his suit, brought an involuntary tremor. Had it not been for the tightly-compressed lips, Fiona could have imagined that he was eager for the ceremony that would make them man and wife to take place, but one glance at the frowning face dispelled all such fantasy. She looked away, pretending an interest in the heavily framed portraits of long-dead City dignitaries that lined the walls. Today might be her wedding day, but it was also no more than the day that she was to fulfil to the letter, but nothing more, the contract that had been drawn up between them in Mr Kilgour's office.

Mr Kilgour was there, his face set in disapproving

lines. He had brought his secretary, Miss Diamond, to be the only other witness to the ceremony and, surprisingly, on their arrival, he had presented Fiona with a bouquet. It was a small posy of gardenias and white heather, lying now on her lap, a tiny oasis of fragrance in the otherwise sterile atmosphere.

Even Fiona's dress was hardly suitable for a bride. Unwilling to alert Janet to the fact that Ian was driving her to Edinburgh for more than another business meeting with the solicitor, she had chosen a cream silk suit from her existing wardrobe, unaware of its effect on the startling blue of her eyes and the softly waving dark auburn of her hair. High bronze pumps brought her to the level of Ian's eyes and she had dreamed of a quick flash of admiration when she had walked slowly down the stairs of Craighill to find him already waiting for her in the kitchen.

The double doors to the inner office were suddenly opened and an usher was beckoning them through. To the end of her life, Fiona was unable to recall the appearance of the registrar who married them. She stood, as if in a trance, listening to the formal words of the civil ceremony, responding automatically and feeling the sudden pressure of the ring upon her finger. A brief warmth as Ian's lips brushed her cheek in response to the instruction to 'Kiss the bride!' and they were married.

The champagne wedding breakfast that Mr Kilgour had insisted upon was a travesty and drained Fiona's fragile emotional resources to the point where she had lost the battle against exhaustion well before Ian had driven them beyond Edinburgh's city limits.

'We're home!' Ian's voice brought her up sharply through the layers of sleep. Her neck was cricked. She had slept with her head against his shoulder and her cheek bore the imprint of his suit. Crumpled and vulnerable for once, she sat up, looking about her like a newly-woken child. They were back at Craighill.

'Would you like me to come in with you, Mrs Hamilton?'

For a moment, she thought she heard a note of tenderness in Ian's voice, but then the sound of her new name brought back all the painful memories of a day which should have meant so much but in fact meant—nothing.

'No!' She spoke abruptly, knowing that she must get away from the masculine presence that even now was stirring her senses and threatening her with betrayal. She fumbled with the door catch, very conscious of the eyes that were watching her in the agonisingly long seconds before the door responded to her trembling fingers and she could stumble out into the cool evening air. The setting sun was dropping in a flaring red and she stood, breathing deeply to regain her composure, the tension in her body outlined against the silhouette of Craighill.

The view of the house and the distant moorland that she had sacrificed her future to maintain was obscured as Ian came towards her. He moved slowly and deliberately and, as he looked at her, she was aware of a desperate tension hanging between them, vibrating like a finely strung wire to the power of an unseen force.

Suddenly she was in his arms. Without seeming to move, he had drawn her to him, gently at first but then with an increasing urgency as his mouth found hers and his fingers moved caressingly down the length of her spine, drawing her body irresistibly close.

The longing that had grown inside her during the days and nights leading up to their marriage could no longer be denied, and a sudden languor weighted her limbs with desire. Her skin burned under the touch of his lips on her cheeks, her eyes, her hair. She sighed, arching her neck and leaning back against the encircling steel of his arms as he kissed the small pulse at the base of her throat into throbbing vibrant life. The longing to caress the crisp darkness of his hair, to give herself completely and utterly to the ecstasy of his love, became almost overwhelming. Then a still small voice of warning crested the rising tide of passion.

Stiffening, she tore herself away from his arms. 'How dare you!' she cried.

'How dare I what?' His tone was easy. 'How dare

I show my wife that I find her a beautiful and desirable woman?'

'No!' Fiona barely registered the words. 'How dare you play with me! How dare you pretend that what we went through this morning was any more than a business arrangement—a sham—a mockery!'

She longed to scream, to strike him, to rail and beat against his sudden rocklike hardness. Instead, with a gasping sob, she turned and ran along the side of the house, her footsteps echoing against the massive walls and her breath coming in harshly tortured bursts. It seemed eternity before she reached the corner and was hidden from his sight.

Instinct stopped her at the kitchen door. It would not do to go in and face Janet in her distressed and flustered state. Nor would it do to go in wearing the thin gold band on the third finger of her left hand.

Slowly she slipped off the ring and held it up against the last of the evening light. It was so small, and yet the whole of her life now seemed to be contained within its tiny circumference.

Although it was so small, the ring hung heavily between Fiona's breasts. Acting on an impulse that she barely understood, she had slipped it on to a thin gold chain the morning after her wedding, and clasped it around her neck. Safely hidden under the soft blue lambswool of her sweater, its occasional movement brought a swift stab of reminder throughout the day.

Dreading her first meeting with Ian, she had gone down to breakfast early to get the ordeal behind her. For once he was late and her mouth was dry with suspense by the time the door finally opened and the man who was now her husband appeared.

'Good morning.' He greeted her quietly, as though nothing out of the ordinary had happened between them, and sat down at the table with the air of a man who had no more than the satisfaction of a hearty appetite on his mind.

Half-way through his meal, he looked up.

'If you've got nothing better to do this morning,' he said, 'there's some paper work that needs attention and I thought we might go into the old laird's office after breakfast and deal with it.' The voice was cool, completely businesslike, and the eyes regarding her across the table were quite expressionless.

'Of course!' Fiona was careful to match his neutral tone and look. There was no need to let him know that she was strangely apprehensive at the prospect of a whole morning to be spent alone in his company. Anyway, it would be good to have the work to occupy her mind.

The farm office was on the other side of the house and their footsteps echoed eerily as they crossed the wide marble expanse of the empty hall. Ian leaned forward and opened the office door, careful not to brush against her, and the space he left between the chairs that he pulled up to the broad, old-fashioned desk made it quite clear that although he intended that they should be able to work comfortably side by side, he had no desire for any accidental contact.

In fact, her husband obviously intended that they should be 'as strange as if they had been married a great while and as well-bred as if they had not been married at all'. The old tag from her schooldays came accurately enough to Fiona's mind. Who had written it? She forced her memory to work. Congreve! That was it! A brilliant, materialistic, eighteenth-century playwright, as little interested in love—true love—as the man at her side.

Ian began to lay out a number of businesslike files on the desk and Fiona's awareness of his physical presence was forgotten as the morning progressed and she became increasingly absorbed with the work in front of them. It took the sight of a long brown index finger, pointing to the space at the front of an official-looking document where she was to sign her name next to his, to remind her of the fact that she was his wife.

'Fiona Montrose Hamilton.' How natural it seemed to be writing it. How much and yet how tantalisingly little it meant.

'This is Simpson's lease.' The crisp efficiency of Ian's voice halted the dangerous drift of her thoughts. 'He has the farm down on the south boundary. Do you remember it?'

Fiona closed her eyes to visualise a small grey stone farmhouse, no different from the rest but set close to a shallow stream that ran laughing over its

pebble bed to join the River Tweed. She also recalled a dour-faced man and his wife and two—no,
three—children, looking at her suspiciously when
she had held out her hand at the tenants' reception.
How could people who lived in a setting of such
beauty remain so cold and impervious? she remembered thinking at the time.

Ian rustled the papers, bringing her back to the
present and the reality of the small, dark office.

'Yes, I remember,' she said. 'When's the lease due
for renewal?'

'Oh, not until Lammas—the first of August,' Ian
explained, 'but I wanted to settle it early because
Simpson'll not be able to pay his rents.'

'Why not?' Alistair Simpson had looked like a
hard worker and certainly not a man to fritter his
money away.

'His child had an accident and not all the costs
could be met out of the National Health Insurance.'
Ian explained. 'She was badly burned and needed
a lot of cosmetic plastic surgery and extra care.
Alistair'll have been behind for—oh, some two years
now. It's all a wee bit complicated, but basically
there's a guaranteed loan out with the bank until
the arrears are made up and he can start again with
a fresh slate.'

'But surely we could afford to forgo the money?—
I mean, forget about the debt?' Fiona asked. She
had, after all, gone through with her fantastic marriage for the sake of tenants like the Simpsons.

'My dear Fiona!' He raised his eyebrows, but it was his gently unexpected use of her name that turned Fiona's heart. 'I can see that you've a lot to learn about your tenants! A man like Alistair Simpson would die rather than accept what he considered to be charity. No, if money alone could have taken care of his problems, they would have been taken care of long ago.'

He riffled through the papers in the file in front of them and held out a cheque on which Fiona could make out her great-uncle's signature. The cheque had never been cashed.

'I doubt the old laird ever had a more uncomfortable five minutes in his life than when he sent this cheque to help with the hospital bills and Alistair brought it back to demand an explanation.' Ian shook his head. 'No, tenants they may be, but they'll bow to no man. Their pride won't let them.'

Pride! The last piece of the jigsaw puzzle that was her marriage slid smoothly into place with a sickening certainty. If pride would not let Alistair Simpson accept a gift from the uncle, how much less likely it was to allow the man called the 'young master' to remain a mere employee of the niece. Ian had not just married her to save Craighill, he had married her to become its master and his signature on the documents alongside hers was proof that he had got his way!

The sound of a chair scraping harshly back cut through Fiona's unpleasant thoughts and the shadow that fell across her was dark as the man who had made himself her husband stood and towered above her. Remembering the isolation of the office, she drew back apprehensively in her chair. By their marriage he had achieved mastery over the estate— might he now be demanding it of her?

Aware of her slight movement, Ian laughed, thin lips curved sensuously back in mock amusement.

'Oh, don't worry, my dear wife!' In one stroke he destroyed the easy working relationship that had grown between them during the morning with the stinging sarcasm of his voice. 'I have no intention of forcing myself upon you! I merely thought that we'd worked long enough and it was time we went for lunch!'

CHAPTER SIX

EXCEPT for those rare moments of dry humour, Ian's way of treating Fiona with a detached courtesy was so complete that there were times when she wanted to scream. The worst moments were when she caught Janet looking at them as though the little housekeeper had by no means abandoned her dreams of the day when there would once more be children to fill the great nurseries of Craighill. But what chance was there of children—at least, her and Ian's children—when the sports car continued to be parked outside the factor's lodge night after night? Fiona thought grimly.

If only she could stop loving him, it would not be so bad, but it only took the sight of her husband's tall figure in the distance to fan the small bright flame inside her into all-consuming life. Apart from chance meetings, their early morning breakfast was the only time they met; Ian had stopped coming to the big house for his evening meal.

The long May days stretched emptily ahead and, with some idea of turning it into a pony-trekking centre, Fiona had decided to open up the big house. She had also entered Blue Fire for the three-day event at Peebles, the nearest large Border town. But the first work to be done on the house was the ripping up and installation of a new central heating system, and the horse trials were not until the end of the month.

The workmen in the house did not appreciate Fiona's presence and the care of Blue Fire had been taken away from her. Although he was still as taciturn and unresponsive as ever, old Sim had taken Blue Fire to his heart and Fiona could sense him growling jealously if she even as much as picked up a curry-comb to groom the horse.

Ian did not seem sympathetic. 'Remember, Sim was your uncle's groom in the old days,' he said one day when she had surprised him in the barn in which Blue Fire was stabled. 'It's natural that he wants to look after the horse, and it's best to let him have his way.'

With that cold comfort he strode off across the yard and Fiona flung the curry-comb on to the floor. Everything was the 'old days'! What about the future—and particularly what about the future of one Fiona Montrose!

One afternoon, Blue Fire exercised and the prospect of spending yet another four hours alone in her room reading until supper time more than she could bear Fiona decided to drive into Melrose. She had been there before, wandering through the ruins of the fine Cistercian abbey and leaning on the bridge to watch the clear brown waters of the Tweed flowing on their way to the sea, but she had never gone there to find the house in which her grandfather had lived and her father had been born.

Her grandfather had been Sir Hector's younger brother, destined by the fate of a Victorian younger son to take up the practice of the law and live in comparative obscurity away from the family estate. Fiona parked her car at the foot of the tall stone column in the town square, with its weatherworn heraldic beast prancing on top, and set off in search of her grandfather's house. With the street name and number memorised, it did not take her long to find the house in a town the size of Melrose, but when she got there there was something familiar about it.

'No, not about the house,' she murmured to herself as she looked at it. 'Something about its surroundings.'

But whatever the something was that tugged so tantalisingly at the strings of her memory, it refused to be identified. Fiona shrugged. Maybe her father had shown her a picture of the place when she had been a child and it was this that had struck a hidden chord of memory in her mind.

The house itself was small and undistinguished. Built in the last century of dull red brick, it had sash windows and the television aerial fixed to the chimney on its steeply pitched slate roof gave it a curiously top-heavy appearance. Even so, the whole place could not have been more than a tenth of the size of Craighill, and Fiona stood and pondered the accident of birth that had left one brother in possession of a mansion and the other with what was little more than a labourer's cottage. The only thing her great-uncle and her grandfather had seemed to have in common was that they had both died lonely and frustrated men, and Fiona shivered at the thought of family history repeating itself in her own marriage.

She was still standing at the gate, dwelling on the web of coincidence that had brought herself and Ian so slowly but inevitably together, when the front door of the cottage opened and a girl began to walk towards her down the path. One look and Fiona knew why she had had the uncanny feeling that she had seen the house before, except that it was not the house that was familiar but the sports car parked outside. That was the same low-slung model that she had seen parked night after night outside the factor's lodge. Without the benefit of daylight she had never realised that it was a pale primrose yellow, but it was definitely the same car, and that meant that the woman coming down the path towards her must be Isobel Carstairs.

Fiona studied the girl who had been a part of her husband's life long before she herself had come to Craighill and was likely to remain a part of it long after she had left. Isobel, she saw, was everything that she had yearned to be when she had been a gawky teenager—small, petite, with elfin features and widely spaced brown eyes, moving with the grace and assurance of a woman who is accustomed to being admired. From the top of her shining dark head to the soles of her handmade shoes, Isobel Carstairs radiated an aura of expensive, self-confident taste.

'Excuse me!' Absorbed in her inspection of Isobel, Fiona had not realised that the other girl had reached the gate and was waiting to be allowed to pass.

'Oh, I'm sorry!' Conscious of every one of her sixty-eight inches, she moved to one side.

With a half nod of acknowledgement, Isobel walked past, but when she was almost at the car she stopped and turned.

'Is there anything you want?' she enquired in a voice that spoke of years of expensive English boarding school education. There was something about it that demanded a swift reply and, irritated with the compulsion that made her hasten to obey, Fiona began to blurt out an explanation for her presence.

'Oh, no, I don't want anything,' she said. 'I was only looking at the house because it used to belong to my grandfather, and my father was born here, so I thought I might just come and. . . .'

Isobel interrupted her. 'So *you're* Fiona Montrose!' She moved a step closer and the look of slightly condescending curiosity gave way to a much franker interest. 'How do you do? I'm Isobel Carstairs.'

'Yes, I know who you are.' Still slightly at a loss, Fiona blurted out the first thing that came into her mind.

'You do?' Isobel accepted the recognition as no more than her due.

'Well, I didn't exactly *know* until just now,' Fiona stumbled on, feeling gauche by comparison with so much cool elegance, 'but I've seen your car up at the lodge and Ian's mentioned you once or twice.'

'Has he indeed!'

'Yes—but I didn't realise that you lived here, though,' Fiona added.

'Oh, that!' Isobel waved away the modest existence of the cottage with a careless gesture. 'That's not mine. It belongs to my uncle. He's a doctor, retired and wanting somewhere quiet to live after years in Harley Street. I only came here for a visit, but the way things have turned out, I've stayed longer than I intended.' Her brilliant lips curved in a self-satisfied smile and she shot a spiteful glance at Fiona from under dark, mascaraed lashes. 'I find the —er—*air* so stimulating!'

To say nothing of the masculine company, Fiona thought savagely. Particularly that of one man—*her* husband! Wounded pride, the result of long nights spent waiting for Isobel's car to leave the factor's lodge, gave her the confidence to join in the game of veiled allusion on which Isobel had embarked and she waited for her to continue.

Isobel obliged. 'In fact,' she said smoothly, 'it all suits me so well up here that I may decide to stay permanently.'

'But won't you find the—er—*air*—boring after a while?'

The note of irony in Fiona's voice made Isobel look up sharply. Perhaps this was not as insignificant an opponent as she had thought.

'Oh, no,' she said, 'I shan't find it boring at all. I shan't be living alone, you see. As a matter of fact, I'm thinking of getting married.' She dropped her voice as if to make Fiona her confidante. 'There's a certain obstacle in the way at the moment, but I'm certain that can soon be dealt with and then I shall be married and living some way out of town. The air is even richer and more exciting out there, don't you think!'

All the old malice was back as the shaft went home and Fiona was aware that Isobel's shrewd eyes were taking in every change of expression.

'I'd love to stay and talk some more,' Isobel went on, 'but I'm rather late for an appointment. Oh!' She turned as though a thought had suddenly occurred to her. 'Maybe I can give you a lift? We're probably going in the same direction.'

'No—no, thank you. I have my own car in the square.' Fiona refused automatically, watching Isobel settle herself behind the wheel and tie a scarf round her shining head to protect it from the breeze.

The implications of what she had just heard were too awful to contemplate. She could not, would not believe that Ian had been so cruel as to tell Isobel about their marriage and the purely business reasons for it, but what else could Isobel's reference to 'obstacles' mean?

The only possible explanation was that Ian had wanted Isobel to know everything so that she would be prepared to wait until he could find some way of having the marriage annulled. Then he could take his rightful place as master of Craighill, but with Isobel at his side.

Chilled and humiliated in the bright spring sunshine, Fiona stood and watched Isobel start the engine of the sports car into life and take off down the road. It was not until the car had disappeared around the corner that she realised that the bright pink headscarf streaming in the breeze was the scarf that had been lying on the coffee table in the factor's lodge when Ian had proposed.

Isobel had driven off in the direction of Craighill and Fiona had expected to see her car when she got there, but there was no sign of it, either near the house or in its usual parking spot outside the factor's lodge.

The more she thought about it, the more its absence puzzled her. Had Isobel been telling the truth, or had her thinly veiled hints about her eventual marriage to Ian merely been barbs designed to wound and scare away a potential rival for the attentions of one of the most eligible men in the district?

Whatever else she might be, Isobel was clearly no fool and she must have heard that, although Craighill had been willed to Fiona, Ian had still inherited Sir Hector's considerable fortune.

Another thing that did not quite match up with Isobel's story was that Ian never seemed to go to her. Surely if he was as much in love with her as she would like to make out, he would take every opportunity to go to Melrose to be at her side. Yet he never did. It was always Isobel who came to the factor's lodge while Ian stayed firmly at Craighill.

Fiona's heart began to flutter. Maybe, just maybe, the situation was not as hopeless as Isobel would like her to believe.

Anyway, it would do no harm to find out what Janet knew. She would have to be careful not to arouse the housekeeper's suspicions, but any hint would be better than this perpetual state of agonising uncertainty.

For all her resolution, Fiona was half-way through her evening meal before she could find the courage to ask her questions. Prying was not something that came easily and she was keenly aware that the answers she received might well not be the ones she wanted.

'I saw Miss Carstairs when I was in Melrose this afternoon,' she remarked finally.

'Who?' Concentrating on getting her pie out of the oven, Janet did not look up. A good sign, Fiona thought. Surely if there had been anything between her favourite and another woman, Janet would have shown more interest, pie or not.

'Miss Carstairs—Isobel Carstairs,' Fiona went doggedly on. 'I believe she's a friend of Mr Hamilton's.' She held her breath.

'Then that'll be the young woman coming to the cottage night after night and keeping the young master from my good food!' Janet said sharply, thumping the pie dish down on the table. 'What my old mother would have said about a lassie chasing after a man like that, I'll never know! Not that she ever shows her face in this house,' she added fiercely, hunting for a knife to cut the pie. 'She knows well enough that she'd get the rough side of my tongue if she did—with her a married woman and all!' She cut the pie and handed Fiona her plate.

'She's married?' Fiona had to struggle not to give herself away.

'Well, divorced more like,' Janet admitted. 'And looking for another man to keep her, no doubt! No, the sooner yon fancy lassie's back in London where she belongs, the better for all of us—the young master included! Now will you be having some cream with your pie, Miss Montrose?' She switched subjects, the cream jug poised expectantly over Fiona's plate.

'Please!' Fiona replied. Plain apple pie had never tasted so delicious, she thought a second later.

But by the time she had finished her dessert her optimism had evaporated. It was all very well to have Janet on her side, but she knew Ian well enough to know that he would not be influenced by his housekeeper's disapproval and, no matter how much the puritanical folk along the Border might disapprove of divorce, in the modern world outside very little notice was taken of it—especially when two people were in love.

Unable to bear the suspense any longer, Fiona made up her mind. After supper she would take Bowser for a walk and, if Isobel's car had arrived outside the cottage, she would accept that everything that Isobel had hinted at was true. It was the same sort of superstition that had kept her hopping over the cracks in the pavement for months when she had been a child, but if the car was there she would know that Isobel had been telling the truth. Ian had not only told her everything but he was only waiting until the estate was secure so that he could get his freedom and marry the woman he really loved!

But if the car was not there? Fiona's mouth went dry. If Isobel's car was not there, she promised herself, she would somehow find the courage to go in and confront her husband.

Bowser had taken himself off on business of his own by the time Fiona turned the corner and stood on the grassy verge across from the lodge. Her heart beat faster. There was no car. The lights were on, but there was no sign of any car. Equally, there was no way of telling who might be inside. She hesitated. She would be rash to go knocking on the door until she had made sure that Ian was alone. She walked a few steps on, unwilling to be seen watching the cottage but straining her ears for the sound of voices. All was silence. Not a sound, not a breath of wind disturbed the overall evening stillness.

'Do you want something?' asked a familiar voice. Absorbed in her preoccupation with the house, Fiona had not been aware of Ian's sudden presence.

'Oh, no, thank you.' She replied unthinkingly, startled by the unexpected sound of his voice so close to her ear.

'In that case, I won't stop.' He began to move on towards the cottage.

'No, please, don't go!' Fiona put out a restraining hand to touch him and he paused, raking her reddening face with angry eyes.

'My dear Fiona,' he said eventually, 'you really must stop behaving like a silly schoolgirl!' He raised his voice in bantering mimicry. 'Come—go! Touch me—don't touch me! It's time you grew up, woman!'

His heavy sarcasm shattered her. What a fool she had been to come! What a fool not to realise that the time when they could have discussed anything was already far in the past.

'Although you may be immature emotionally,' he went on, eyes dropping from her face to the swelling curve of her breasts, 'you are no longer a child but a woman and, as such, you should be able to understand just how provocative your behaviour is. But maybe I'm wrong!' He laughed and Fiona had never been more conscious of the untamed quality running just beneath the surface of his personality. 'Maybe you are only too aware of that fact!'

He drew her to him, harshly, possessively, but before she had the time to struggle, a scream ripped through the air and froze them both. It was accompanied by a low rumble of menace which at first Fiona could not identify. Then she realised that she was listening to Bowser growling.

Running footsteps crashed through the shrubbery behind them and then a clearly terrified Isobel emerged from the screen of laurel bushes with Bowser loping noiselessly by her side. His fangs were exposed in a silent snarl and he was no longer the good-natured pet but a primitive, fierce watchdog.

'Ian!' Isobel's voice broke with relief. She rushed across the narrow strip of grass and flung herself into his arms, babbling out an almost incoherent explanation about a flat tire and losing her way as she had walked through the grounds of Craighill.

Unnoticed by either of them, Fiona caught hold of Bowser's collar and turned away. She had seen enough. The sight of Ian bending protectively over the tiny figure in his arms had told her everything that she had wanted to know. This was how a man behaved towards the woman he loved; tender, cherishing, not wounding with heavy sarcasm. What Isobel had told her was true: she had no option now but to believe it. It was Isobel that Ian loved; the evidence had been there before her eyes just a few seconds earlier. All that was left for her was a hollow mockery of a marriage and a pride that would let no one see the hot tears scalding her eyes.

In the days that followed there were times when Fiona felt like the Snow Maiden. Shock lent everything an air of unreality and she felt as though she was imprisoned in ice, fully aware of what was going on and yet unable by word or gesture to alter the direction of her life.

She should have confronted Ian and demanded an explanation. She should have gone to Mr Kilgour and asked about an annulment of her marriage. But she could do neither. All she could do was to allow herself to be swept along on the tide of events that had brought her to this point.

Ian no longer came to the house not even for breakfast, and Janet was concerned.

'That great girl from the farm won't be looking after him properly,' she repeated darkly. 'My old mother would turn in her grave if she could see the goings-on in this house!'

Janet's disgust barely registered. Nothing really

registered any more, not even the sight of Ian in the distance. Even that failed to rouse Fiona's emotions.

The only time she came alive was on the back of Blue Fire. The three-day event was rushing towards them and the mare was a complete novice. Fiona schooled and exercised her until she fell into bed exhausted every night, to sleep the moment her head touched the pillow, untroubled and unaware of anyone coming or going to the factor's lodge.

Bursting with fitness under Sim's possessive care, and tormented by the insects brought out by the warmer weather, Blue Fire was becoming a difficult ride. There were times when Fiona wished that the complicated dressage test, which had to be committed to memory for the first day of the event, included the capriole, the superb flying leap performed by the stallions of the Spanish Riding School in Vienna. She was sure that the mare would have taken much more readily to that than to the precision of the collected trot and counter-canter included in the dressage test to test her suppleness and obedience.

Shifted in the saddle one morning by an enormous buck, Fiona decided to abandon dressage for the day and let the horse work off some of her excess energy in a gallop along the tops. The air was cooler up on the moors and there were fewer insects to bother them both and make Blue Fire sweat and fidget until the foam fell from her bit on to her flecked shoulders and gave her dapple grey coat the dull sheen of iron.

They were on their way home when a cock pheasant took off in front of them in a whirring blur of red and emerald green, startling them both. The mare broke into a crazy gallop and, for a moment, Fiona thought that she had lost control. They were almost at the house before the horse came back to her and she had only a glimpse of the red sports car parked out in front before it was obscured by the outbuildings and the trees.

Her first reaction was that it was Isobel's. It had the same sleek sporty lines, but the colour was wrong. It was a bright dark red instead of Isobel's supremely feminine primrose yellow. In fact, Fiona realised with a start of surprise, the car outside Craighill looked very much like the one she had last seen locked up in the garage underneath Geoff Gilson's mews cottage in Kensington.

Fiona had not given her former landlord a thought for days. When she had heard of her inheritance she had written to Geoff and to his solicitor, asking if she could be released from her lease of the tiny cottage. The solicitor had replied, cancelling it, but there had been no word from Geoff, which, at the time, had seemed strange.

Ever since Geoff had gone to Africa, airmail letters had been arriving with surprising frequency. Their tone suggested something more personal than the relationship that normally exists between landlord and tenant and, when Geoff had suggested that they might keep in touch when he came back to

London, Fiona realised that she must have made more of an impression than she had realised in her two meetings with the easy-going civil engineer.

She walked Blue Fire into the yard and swung herself down. Sim was already at the horse's head and he ran a disapproving hand along her neck. The mare whickered softly in response.

'She'll be a bit warm,' Sim commented.

'I'm afraid we've had our moments this morning!' Fiona was so used by now to the yard man's perpetual disapproval that she could let it wash over her. 'We walked the last half-mile, but you know what a handful she is! You should, because it's your good care that's made her so fit!'

Even this tribute failed to win a smile. 'Aye, and she'll need to be, too, if she's to trounce them all at Peebles,' was all Sim said.

Fiona accepted defeat. Much as Sim obviously approved of Blue Fire, it was clear that he would never approve of her owner. With an inward shrug, she watched him lead the horse across the yard and then turned away, wondering if it really was Geoff Gilson's car that she had seen parked outside the house.

It was. Fiona opened the kitchen door and there was Geoff sitting in old Sir Hector's chair by the side of the empty old-fashioned range, Bowser's head adoringly in his lap, the picture of contentment. The only discordant note was Janet hovering ominously in the background.

'Fiona!' Gently pushing Bowser to one side, Geoff got to his feet, deeply tanned and looking even more like an overgrown teddy bear than Fiona had remembered.

'Geoff!'

Suddenly she was in his arms, and how good it felt. No tensions, no complications, just the warmth of his arms around her and the rough fabric of his jacket against her head. This could have been the brother she had never had.

'He told me that you knew him, otherwise I should never have let him in.' Janet was determined to make her disapproval perfectly clear. 'The old laird would never permit strangers in the house—but I can see now well enough that you're not strangers, so I'll be about my work!' She picked up her duster and disappeared, shutting the door behind her with a decided click.

'My, what a welcome!' Geoff took no notice but looked at Fiona, smiling: no taller than she but broad and heavily built.

Fiona laughed, blushing slightly as she disentangled herself from his arms.

'Blame Bowser!' she said. 'Living with your dog makes me feel that you're one of the family. Purely platonically, of course!'

'Oh, I see.'

Did she imagine the quick flash of disappointment in Geoff's eyes? Fiona wondered.

'But Geoff, what are you doing here?' she went on

quickly. 'I didn't expect you back from Africa for at least another three months. I thought you said that the bridge you were building wasn't going to be finished until the autumn. What went wrong?'

'In a nutshell, too much water and not enough bridge!' he joked. 'No, seriously, the whole scheme was much too premature. A lot more planning needs to be done before we can even start on the first stage, and planning's what I've been sent back to England to do. Meanwhile, I've got two glorious weeks' holiday and I was hoping to persuade you to spend them with me—with Bowser as chaperone, of course.'

'Oh, Geoff, I can't!' Was it just the three-day event that stopped her or something—someone—else? Fiona could not be sure.

'I see.'

'No, you don't!' The look of sudden rejection on Geoff's face was more than Fiona could bear. It was so like Bowser. In fact, that was what they were, she realised, a pair: a big, shaggy dog and a big, shaggy man.

'I've got Blue Fire up here,' she explained, 'and I've entered her for a three-day event—a horse show,' she translated for the benefit of his puzzled expression. 'So I can't leave, but why don't you stay? If you don't mind roughing it a bit, I've got seventeen empty bedrooms in various states of disrepair. You can take your pick!'

Geoff hesitated and she sensed intuitively that he

was turning her suggestion over in his mind, wondering if he could accept it on the basis of the friendship that was all she was offering. He finally decided.

'Great!' he said. 'I'll get my bags from the car and then you can take me on a tour of inspection.' He placed his arm around her shoulders. 'You know, I could hardly believe it when I got your letter telling me that you'd inherited all this.' He waved his arm to take in the whole of Craighill and then returned it fondly to Fiona's shoulder. 'It took ages to reach me because I'd gone up-country and when it arrived, I knew that I was coming home, so I thought that rather than write I'd surprise you and come here straight away....'

Fiona felt rather than heard Ian's entrance to the room, and Geoff's voice, too, trailed away as he became aware of the sudden chill in the air. It was a chill that had nothing to do with the half-opened back door. Ian was in the doorway, his tall frame outlined against a background of the open moorland, and his steely grey eyes took in the scene in front of him with one barely perceptible glance.

And what a scene of happy reunion it must appear, Fiona realised—herself flushed and happy, Geoff with his arm fondly round her shoulders and Bowser adoringly at their feet.

'I'm sorry, I'm interrupting.' Ian spoke through thinly compressed lips, already about to leave.

'No, don't go.' Fiona stopped him in mid-departure. Why, oh, why had he chosen to put in an appearance at just this moment? she thought. He had not been near the house for days, but just when Geoff's unexpected arrival had thawed the cloak of icy indifference with which she had protected herself ever since she had seen him gather Isobel so tenderly to him—just at the moment when her defences were down and the mere sight of him was enough to send a fresh thrill of yearning surging through her—her husband had appeared, to find her in another man's arms.

'I'd like you to meet Geoff Gilson,' she began. 'I knew him from when—I mean, I knew him in London.' She stumbled on, aware that she was making the situation worse with every word. 'Geoff, this is Ian Hamilton, my——' Husband! The word trembled on her lips, but she bit it back. 'My estate manager,' she said.

'Hi!' Geoff's casual greeting fell like a stone into the strained silence and Ian ignored both the man and his outstretched hand.

'I came to see Macbeth,' he said. 'Tell her to come over to the lodge later, will you?'

'He's pretty high-handed, isn't he?' Geoff asked when the door had closed behind Ian's unyielding back. 'I say, are you all right?'

Willing herself into a semblance of normality, Fiona forced a smile.

'Yes, I'm fine,' she said. 'Let's go and get your luggage and see about finding you a room.'

CHAPTER SEVEN

IF Ian had been distant since their marriage, after Geoff's arrival he became invisible. Except for the fact that Craighill continued to run with clockwork efficiency, there might have been no estate manager.

There were times when Fiona longed to go to him, to explain to him that the conclusion he had reached when he had seen her in Geoff's arms had been wrong, but pride always stopped her—pride and the memory of his dark head bent protectively over the tiny, terrified figure of Isobel. Let him go to Isobel for comfort, Fiona told herself. He had already made it clear that it was Isobel he preferred, so why should she risk the anger that she had seen written in his face by trying to convince him that Geoff was just a friend?

It was so unfair! Ian could marry her, knowing that he was already in love with another woman, but for her to be seen with another man brought all sorts of unspoken accusations.

The suspicions were certainly in Janet's mind. No matter how hard Geoff tried to win her round, the housekeeper remained stubbornly set against him, and the pattern was set from his very first morning at Craighill.

'That was a splendid breakfast, Janet!' Geoff

finished the last slice of toast and marmalade and gave her one of his warm, infectious smiles.

'It's only a proper meal for a working man,' Janet said dourly, unimpressed by both the smile and the compliment. 'The pity of it is that the one man who needs it is not here to have it.' She shot a glance at Ian's empty chair before switching to another favourite tack. 'And I don't know either what the old laird would have said if he could have lived to see breakfast dishes on the table at ten o'clock in the morning!'

'Oh, Janet, it's only for once!' Fiona tried to soften her, but Janet was not to be won.

'We'll see about that!' she said darkly. 'And now I can't stand here gossiping all day—I've got work to do even if others haven't.'

She was still grumbling even after the door had closed behind her and she was half way up the back stairs. Geoff grinned.

'I don't seem to be making too good an impression on the natives! First your estate manager—and now Janet,' he said.

'Oh, don't worry,' Fiona replied. 'What you've seen is nothing compared to the reception that I always get from the yard man. If Sim had his way, no lassie—and a Sassenach lassie at that—would ever have been allowed to take the place of the old laird!' She attempted an imitation of Sim's Lowland accent and failed miserably.

'Changing the subject, that's something I've been

meaning to ask you,' said Geoff. 'With your uncle being a laird, I thought you'd be a lady at the very least.'

'Oh, no—the title died with my uncle. It was a baronetcy—laird was just the courtesy title that they used round here. It's a shame really, because it had been in the family for more than three hundred years. One of my ancestors got it from James the First, but it couldn't be inherited by a woman. Another example of male supremacy, I suppose!' Fiona laughed, wishing that the arrogant masculine face figure that had appeared in her mind's eye bore more resemblance to her uncle than to the man who was undoubtedly, if unwillingly, her husband.

But with Geoff's company to distract her, she let the days pass by, trying not to think about her future or the man who held it in the palm of his hand. Geoff had chosen the big bedroom in the front tower for his stay, and this was the room that Fiona had earmarked for her own when the house had been renovated and she could move out of her uncle's old quarters.

She had had his room fixed up as a temporary bedsitter, with bookshelves and a portable television set, but she was looking forward to the day when she could move into the sunny master bedroom over the front entrance with its view across the moors to the distant Cheviot and Eildon Hills.

The small dressing-room leading from it would be perfect as a nursery, she had thought, remember-

ing the awful suite of little rooms hidden away on
the attic floor. There would be no banishment to
that prison-like atmosphere for her children. But
that had been before Ian had rejected her completely: before she had discovered his love for Isobel. Now, with the certain knowledge that the little
dressing-room would never be used for their children, the bedroom's main attraction was that the
factor's lodge could be seen from neither of its tall
stone arched windows.

Once the new central heating system had been
installed, renovations to the house had begun to pro-
ceed with surprising rapidity and, apart from its
new carpet and curtains, the master bedroom had
been the first room to be finished.

Fiona had decided on an overall colour scheme of
creams and golds for the house: colours which both
lightened the atmosphere and set off the fine pieces
of antique furniture that she intended to keep. She
was satisfied with the results as far as they went, but
something more was needed: a final touch, a flair
for interior decoration that she knew she did not
possess. But Geoff did.

'It's not so far from being a civil engineer and
designing bridges to being an architect and designing houses,' Geoff explained one morning, holding
a small square of brocade up to the light and tug-
ging at it to test its quality and strength. 'And from
building a house to designing its interior is an even
smaller step.'

They were sitting in Sir Hector's old office, the one place in the house that Ian had refused to have altered when Fiona had first broached her plans for redecoration.

'We'll keep it as it is for the old laird's memory,' Ian had said shortly. 'The rest you can do what you like with.'

So the office had remained as it was, dark, with untidily filled bookshelves lining the walls and an outside button-back leather sofa underneath the one window. There had been times, sitting at the old-fashioned desk waiting for inspiration to strike her, when Fiona had wished that she had left everything as it had been in her great-uncle's day, and not just his office. Now, with Geoff at her side, sifting through fabric samples that she had had sent in from Edinburgh, things no longer seemed so hopeless.

Geoff finished looking at the fabric sample and let it drop through his fingers into the wastepaper basket. 'No, I don't think so,' he said.

'Why didn't you go in for it? Architecture or interior design, I mean?' Fiona asked, remembering the exquisite taste of the mews cottage that she had rented from him. With its collection of delicate Coalport figurines, highlighted by the overall decor and so apparently out of character with Geoff's 'hail fellow, well met' personality, she had no doubt that he would have succeeded.

'Two reasons, mainly,' said Geoff. 'First, when

you're a soccer-playing sixteen-year-old, you're a bit reluctant to admit that you're interested in fabric and design in case anyone gets the wrong idea about you and, secondly, around that time I had this fantastic maths teacher and he put the idea of civil engineering into my head.'

'Do you regret it?' Fiona asked.

'Sometimes—but that's all water under the bridge now, as you might say,' Geoff laughed. 'And now, as I don't think anyone could possibly get the wrong impression about me—and I quite frankly don't care if they do!—why don't we take ourselves into Edinburgh tomorrow and see if we can do better than this?'

He picked up the whole pile of fabric samples and dropped them in the rubbish bin.

Fiona was delighted. 'That would be marvellous, Geoff, if you're sure you don't mind,' she said enthusiastically.

'Mind? I'm only too glad to have a chance to indulge myself,' he said. 'You can do fantastic things with a place like this. The entrance hall, for instance. Now that you've got heating in, it can be turned into a place that you really want to spend time in and not just rush through before you freeze to death.'

Talking, they left the office and walked through the house on their way to the front door, Geoff sketching imaginary plans with an enthusiastic hand. The yellow sports car was outside the factor's lodge, Fiona noticed, as they walked along the side of the house to the yard where Blue Fire was waiting to be ridden out on her morning exercise. It was unusual for the car to be there during the day, Fiona thought, but Isobel probably had her reasons for making her proprietorial interest in Ian absolutely clear.

Not that she cared, she told herself dishonestly. Isobel Carstairs could come and go as she pleased, it made not the slightest difference to her.

Geoff left the gravelled path and went back into the shrubbery to get a better view of the towers and turrets of the roof. Fiona joined him. Half hidden in the bushes, not talking, the sound of a woman's voice came clearly towards them.

'As far as I can see, there's absolutely no reason why you shouldn't,' the voice said. 'This old mausoleum is hardly likely to fall down just because you're not here to prop it up for half a day.'

'Isobel, your views as always are exciting, but not always practical.' There was a note of indulgence in Ian's voice, which seemed to annoy the unseen Isobel even more.

'I didn't notice any hesitation when the charming Miss Montrose wanted to be taken into Edinburgh,' she said acidly. 'Oh, well,' she went on in a more threatening tone, 'if you won't come with me, I suppose you won't. But I do assure you, my dear Ian, that there are plenty of men who will!'

Isobel's quick footsteps came rapidly along the

path. Unwilling conspirators in silence, Geoff and Fiona stood back among the bushes as she turned the corner of the house.

Isobel looked lovely, Fiona had to admit that. Dark cap of hair shining, tiny perfect figure taut with anger and the subtle pink of the expensively cut suit reflected in the flushed cheeks. It was clearly unusual for Isobel Carstairs not to get her own way —particularly with men.

'*Who* was that?' Geoff's voice was little more than an indrawn breath of admiration when Isobel had gone past.

'Isobel Carstairs!' Fiona realised that she was echoing Geoff's awed whisper and sharply raised her voice. 'A neighbour,' she added.

The engine of the unseen sports car coughed into life. There was the spatter of gravel as the tires took hold and then Isobel cut off at a recklessly fast pace.

'That seems to be quite a girl!' The half-awed hush of admiration was still in Geoff's voice.

Provoked, Fiona began to walk quickly along the path in the direction of the yard and Blue Fire.

'I don't know about that!' she said tartly over her shoulder. 'But if you want to know more about her, you'll have to ask Ian. She's his friend.'

'Maybe they're not so friendly any more,' Geoff speculated. 'Where did you say she lived?'

'I didn't—but she lives in Melrose, if you really want to know. Just behind the church, as a matter of fact.' If Geoff wanted to tangle with Isobel Carstairs, that was his business, Fiona thought. A few steps on, she stopped, suddenly ashamed of her display of petty jealousy, and waited for him to catch up. 'I'm sorry, Geoff,' she said. 'I must be a bit edgy this morning. A ride'll do me good. Blow the cobwebs away! Forgive me?'

'Of course!' The comforting heaviness of Geoff's arm went around her shoulder and they continued their walk towards the yard where Sim was waiting with an impatient Blue Fire.

Five minutes later, from her vantage point on the mare's back, Fiona could see them both. Geoff walking along the side of the house, head bent in contemplation, and Ian coming out of the barn to have a word with Sim. As she watched, Ian laughed, head thrown back in characteristic fashion, and walked off across the yard with a light and buoyant step. Not at all the demeanour of a man who has just had an argument with the girl he loves, Fiona thought irrationally.

Geoff had taken himself off on his own for most of the rest of that day and when they started the drive to Edinburgh the following afternoon, Fiona put the air of constraint that seemed to hover round him down to her imagination. He had not said anything more about Isobel, and Fiona did not raise the subject. She had no wish to spoil what promised to be a pleasant outing.

Unlike the first time Fiona had been to Edin-

burgh to see the solicitor and discover the draw-
backs to her inheritance, today there were parking
spaces everywhere. They found one easily in a cul-
de-sac leading off Princes Street and when they got
back into the main thoroughfare, Geoff paused and
looked up and down appreciatively.

'It's lovely, isn't it?' he asked.

Fiona had to agree. The grey stone of Edinburgh
gave the city a certain austerity, but there was also
an undeniable grandeur in the long sweep of
Princes Street down from the Scott Memorial past
the ominous bulk of the Castle brooding on its crag.
The tulips blazing in the flower beds reminded
Fiona that the spring that she had left behind in
London when she had driven north to Craighill had
not only arrived in Scotland but was almost over.
And it had been a springtime that had been the
most momentous of her life, with so much crammed
into its few short weeks to change her future for
ever.

Geoff took her arm, bringing her back to the
present with a start. 'Come on,' he said. 'As I remember it, Fingals is just down there and if we're
going to get everything ordered up for the house
this afternoon, we'd better get started.'

Fingals was an expensive department store,
specialising in exclusive furnishing fabrics. Once
in its plushly carpeted interior, Fiona would have
been content with the attentions of an assistant, but
Geoff demanded to see the buyer.

'Then it will be Mr Plummer you want, sir.' The salesman who had come up to them now went scurrying off behind the scenes.

They browsed around the soft furnishing display until a tall young man appeared, clearly irritated at having been summoned to attend to what he assumed to be a routine sale.

'Can I help you, sir?' he asked condescendingly.

'Yes.' By contrast, Geoff was at his most down to earth. 'This is Miss Montrose, the new owner of Craighill. You've probably heard of it—an estate on the Borders. She's interested in having Fingals renovate the entire interior of the house—provided, of course, you can come up with products of a suitable standard—and not like the fabric samples that you've already sent!' he added pointedly.

The buyer was at once all eager deference and attention, and Fiona giggled inwardly at the quick change of expression that had come over his previously haughty face. She was beginning to enjoy herself.

'Of course, sir—madam,' the buyer said. 'Will you come this way?'

He ushered them from the open sales floor into the privacy of his office, his enthusiasm becoming tempered with respect as Geoff produced minutely drawn plans for every room at Craighill, complete with paint samples and detailed measurements. There were even sketches of major items of furniture, and Fiona marvelled at the time and precision that Geoff had devoted to his self-appointed task.

Her admiration increased as salespeople were summoned to the office to struggle in under bolts of material and the buyer himself made arrangements to visit Craighill. This was the sort of thing that her Aunt Madeline could have done: gone to the top, demanded the best, but Fiona would never have had the confidence.

The home that was emerging from the plans as additional details were sketched in and snips of fabric attached to the paper was more, far more, than she could ever have achieved alone. It was also going to cost far more than she had anticipated, but she put the thought of money resolutely to one side. She had jeopardised her future to save Craighill. Surely that gave her the right to spend what she liked on the house?

Besides, Geoff thought that the money that they were spending was her own. He had assumed that she had come into a substantial fortune with her inheritance, and she could hardly tell him the truth without also disclosing the fact of her extraordinary marriage. And, in a way, what Geoff thought was true. Inheriting Craighill had forced her into marriage, and surely that gave her the right to spend the money that had come with it.

At last they had finished with the buyer and were back on the sales floor.

'What about a cup of tea?' Geoff suggested.

'What, here?' Fiona looked around her, surprised.

'They've a restaurant on the top floor,' said Geoff, pointing to a store guide by the escalator.

Still somewhat surprised that Geoff should want to linger in Fingals, Fiona obediently let him take her to the restaurant, his burly masculine frame incongruous among the feather hats and expensive tweeds of the otherwise almost exclusively female clientele.

'Well, this is nice!' The fragile gilt tea-room chair looked almost on the point of collapse as Geoff leaned back and let his eyes roam around the crowded room.

'Yes, but hardly your style, I should have thought,' Fiona replied, wondering if she was being over-sensitive in suspecting that Geoff had something more than a little afternoon refreshment on his mind.

'Oh, I don't know! A cup of tea's a cup of tea wherever you find it,' Geoff said lightly.

Somehow the attempted nonchalance did not quite succeed and he again seemed slightly embarrassed. No, she thought, 'ill at ease' would be more accurate—unease mixed with an air of expectancy, giving him a slightly abstracted manner, so unlike his usual direct, forthright self. This was the manner, so unlike the manner that she had noticed earlier in the car on their way to Edinburgh.

'You are happy with what we've done, aren't you?' Geoff asked, noticing her silence. 'I mean, fabric and design-wise, you've no second thoughts?'

'No, far from it!' Fiona hastened to reassure him. 'I couldn't have come anywhere near it by myself. I've just not got the knack of visualising things in advance—I mean, colours and so forth. Everything actually has to be in place before I can see. ...' She was stopped in mid-flow by Geoff's quick look of delighted recognition as someone came up behind her.

'Why, what a pleasant surprise!' The voice that floated over her shoulder was full of seductive charm, quite unlike the shrill, angry tones that she had heard the previous day.

It couldn't be! Fiona turned in her chair. It was: Isobel Carstairs. Isobel was standing right behind her looking like the cat who had eaten the cream, beautiful in a coat of springtime yellow with the orange silk scarf at her neck picked up in the colour of her lipstick and accentuating the creamy pallor of her skin so that her widely spaced brown eyes appeared deeper and more mysterious than ever.

'Isobel!' Geoff was quickly on his feet, his pleasure total and undisguised. 'You know Fiona, don't you?' he added, as if suddenly remembering her presence.

'Of course I know Fiona,' Isobel tinkled. 'We met the other day and had such an interesting little heart-to-heart! Girlish chat, you know!'

She laughed again and Fiona sat there, knowing that she must seem gauche and boorish by comparison with so much elegance and charm. Geoff pulled out a chair.

'Won't you join us?' he pleaded.

'Well, just for a moment, then.' Isobel slipped into the tiny gilt chair with precisely the right amount of hesitation.

Geoff sat down and looked imploringly across at Fiona. 'I just happened to bump into Isobel in Melrose yesterday afternoon,' he said, his eyes begging her not to give him away. 'We got talking and when she said that she might be coming into Edinburgh today, I suggested . . . well, I thought we might. . . .'

'So sweet, don't you think! Geoff positively insisted that I try and join you for tea.' Isobel spoke to Fiona, but her eyes were on Geoff. 'Unfortunately, I can't stay long. I've got to go round to the theatre and return two tickets. There's a play that I'm dying to see, but my escort let me down at the last minute, and there's nothing I hate so much as going to the theatre alone.'

'Perhaps we could all go?' Geoff looked hopefully across at Fiona.

'Oh, I doubt it,' Isobel had interrupted before Fiona had a chance to reply. 'The play's a smash hit, so I know I can return my tickets, but I don't think we could possibly get a third.'

'Then why don't you two go together?' Fiona picked up Isobel's obvious cue and entered the conversation for the first time.

'Oh, no, we couldn't possibly do that!' Geoff just

failed to hide the enthusiasm in his voice.

'Why not?' Fiona asked flatly. 'If Isobel's got her car here, I can take yours. I'm quite capable of driving myself home, you know!'

Suddenly all that mattered was that she should be gone. Away from both of them—from the subtly scheming Isobel and Geoff who had fallen so readily under her spell.

'Well, if you're sure....' Geoff's polite resistance was fighting a losing battle against anticipation at spending the evening alone with Isobel.

Fiona got to her feet. 'I'm quite sure,' she said. The brief glint of triumph in Isobel's eyes was nothing compared to Fiona's own determination to end an argument over an issue that was already settled. 'Now, if that's decided, maybe you can get the bill and I can make a start.'

Isobel chose to stay on at Fingals and wait for Geoff while he took Fiona to where the car was parked. He walked her quickly, anxious to be back, but when he had unlocked the door and handed Fiona the key a look of embarrassment settled on his face.

'I hope you believe I didn't plan this?' he said. 'The theatre, I mean?'

'Didn't you?' Fiona settled herself into the driver's seat and adjusted the mirror.

'No, honestly!' Geoff's face was almost comical in his efforts to convince her. 'I did look Isobel up in Melrose yesterday afternoon and I did know that there was a chance that we might bump into her for tea today, but that's as far as it went. Nothing was said about the theatre, and we didn't make any plans.'

'Maybe *you* didn't,' Fiona thought, looking up into the face hovering above her, 'but you can be sure that the lovely Isobel had everything neatly planned out in that shining head of hers!' Then, remembering the argument that they had overheard between Ian and Isobel the previous day, she relented. What chance had Geoff really stood if a scheming little piece like Isobel had decided to use him to get her own back on Ian?

'Oh, all right,' she said. 'I believe you, though thousands wouldn't.'

'Thanks!' Geoff's relief was obvious and he leaned his elbows on the sports car roof to peer down earnestly at her. 'You know, she's not had an easy life, Fiona,' he went on. 'She married this playboy type and he just dumped her. Ran off with another woman without leaving her a penny—and she's got no one, absolutely no one, to turn to.'

Except an obliging uncle with a house in Melrose, Fiona thought caustically, and just about every eligible man she met—particularly if that man seemed to be showing any interest in someone called Fiona Montrose!

'Be careful, Geoff!' She contented herself with a warning; to say anything more would only sound like sour grapes. 'She may not be as helpless or as hard done by as she looks.'

'I will.' Geoff stepped back and Fiona let in the clutch, pleased to be away alone with herself and her thoughts. Her last glimpse of Geoff was in the driving mirror, walking quickly back in the direction of Fingals and Isobel.

The sight acted as an irritant and Fiona drove hard, making the forty winding miles from Edinburgh in well under the hour, and her thoughts kept pace with her driving. The anger and resentment that she had kept damped down in Isobel's presence began to boil inside her. Geoff's weakness over Isobel, understandable though it might be, was the last straw, and by the time Fiona turned in through the gates of Craighill she was in a state of cold, controlled fury such as she had never experienced before.

Ever since her arrival in Scotland, it seemed as if everyone and everything had conspired to dupe her —Geoff, Ian, even Craighill itself. If the estate had not been in such a bad financial state, she would never have got herself trapped into a travesty of a marriage with a man who did not love her and had so little respect for her that he was prepared to carry on an affair with another woman right under her nose. In fact, her only consolation was that, whether he knew it or not, Ian now seemed on the verge of losing Isobel. And once the three-day event was over he would lose Fiona herself, she promised herself. She would leave the house, the estate, Ian—above all Ian—and she would go back to London and try and rebuild the shattered remnants of her life as though this disastrous episode had never happened.

Slamming the car door viciously, she turned and cannoned straight into the man who was uppermost in her thoughts. She had barely seen him since their wedding day, and yet his touch was so familiar that the impact of his hard strength sent an involuntary thrill shuddering through her body. His arms, steadying them both against their sudden collision, were bands of steel around her and she knew that she had to get away if the weakness that threatened her was not to totally engulf her.

'Don't touch me!' she gasped, almost choking on the words.

'My dear Fiona!' There was a mocking tone to his voice. 'Until you literally threw yourself into my arms, I had no intention of touching you—far from it! But now you mention it, it doesn't seem such a bad idea at all.' Instead of loosening, his arms tightened their grip, crushing her against him with a cruelty of which he must have been aware. 'After all,' he murmured silkily against her hair, 'you seem willing enough to bestow your favours elsewhere! Very willing, in fact, judging by the touching little episode I interrupted the other evening. Having seen you in the estimable Mr Gilson's arms, I realise that I was wrong when I questioned your maturity as a woman, and as no matter how much you may detest the fact you are my wife, I see no reason why I should be the only man excluded from your charms!'

'Let go of me!' This was a mood of bitter anger she had never seen him in before. Half frightened, half thrilled, Fiona struggled ineffectually against the strength that held her, her heart fluttering like a caged bird against the rough tweed of his jacket.

Then suddenly, abruptly, there was no more need to struggle. Her husband had released her and a deep longing in her had replaced the pressure of his arms.

'But maybe I shouldn't take advantage of our unexpected meeting,' he said sarcastically. 'Particularly as I hadn't expected it to be you at all. When I saw the car, I thought that our visitor had returned, and I wanted to have a few words with Mr Geoffrey Gilson.'

To warn Geoff away from Isobel, no doubt, Fiona thought, looking up into her husband's hard, set face. He must have somehow found out about their meeting and his immediate instinct had been to confront Geoff and warn him away. Scare him off, if necessary, if the bitterly angry look on Ian's face was any indication of his feelings. Fiona made up her mind. She would not help Geoff and Isobel, but neither would she give her husband any comfort. Let him suffer as he had made her suffer!

'I'm afraid you'll be disappointed if you had

hoped to see Geoff today,' Fiona said carefully. 'He's still in Edinburgh—with a friend.'

'Ah, well, it will wait.' Ian studied her intently, a gleam of mockery returning to his eyes. 'But what's put you in such a bad mood, my dear wife?' he asked eventually. 'Could it be having to drive home alone without Mr Gilson's manly shoulder to rest your pretty head on?'

Fiona's fragile self-control snapped. 'You are despicable!' She raised her hand, but he was quicker, catching her wrist in a vice like grip.

'Am I?' he taunted. 'Or is this display of anger—which I'm sure you are well aware is extremely becoming—merely because I can see through the little game that the pair of you are playing?'

Suddenly the voice had turned to granite, the eyes to slate.

'Game? What game?' Fiona asked.

'Come now, woman! Surely you don't expect me to believe you're as naïve as that? You know perfectly well what I'm talking about!'

The fingers on her wrist relaxed and Fiona snatched it away, massaging it gently to restore the circulation.

'I've no idea what you mean!' she retorted.

For a split second, a shadow of half-belief flashed in the eyes looking down at her, but then it was gone and the granite had returned once more—harsh, impermeable, matching the cutting edge of his voice.

'Whatever other shortcomings you may have, I had at least accounted you honest,' he warned. 'Be careful! You once had my respect. Don't lose it altogether!'

With that he strode away towards the factor's lodge, leaving Fiona baffled, hurt and angry, but uppermost in her mind was complete bewilderment as to what he could mean.

CHAPTER EIGHT

THE County Ball, on the eve of the three-day event at Peebles, was one of the most important social occasions of the year. Traditionally held in one of the great houses along that part of the eastern Border, this year it was to be given by Sir Archie Douglas and his wife in their magnificent home at Blackwoods, an estate running parallel with Craighill.

Had Geoff not been there, Fiona would never have gone. Dancing and celebration were the last things that interested her at that point in time. When, however, the invitation had come with the morning post shortly after his arrival, Geoff had looked across the breakfast table at the heavily embossed invitation card with something akin to awe in his eyes.

'I thought things like that went out with Queen Victoria!' he commented. 'What's it for?'

'The County Ball,' Fiona replied casually, putting the card to one side by her plate.

Geoff noticed her lack of interest. 'Aren't you going?' he asked.

'No, I don't think so.'

'Why not?' Geoff sounded surprised. 'It'll do you good—take you out of yourself. You look a bit peaky, if you don't mind me saying so. Anyway, won't the neighbours think it strange if the newest arrival doesn't put in an appearance?'

'Probably.' Fiona remembered how pressing Lady Douglas had been when she had called a week or so earlier to welcome her to the district and to make sure that she knew about the ball. 'But I really don't feel up to it, and anyway, I haven't got anybody to go with.'

'Yes, you have,' Geoff said promptly. 'Me! And'—he paused with the air of a conjuror about to produce a rabbit from a hat—'it just so happens that I have my dinner jacket with me!'

With Geoff so keen to go, Fiona had been unwilling to deprive him of the one social occasion that it was likely to be in her power to provide during his stay, and she had finally accepted the invitation for both of them. And it was ironic, she thought, dressing in her room on the night of the ball, that for all his former enthusiasm, Geoff now probably wanted to go even less than she did. Or at least, if he did want to go, she amended, teasing a stubborn wisp of hair into place, she was certainly not the partner he would have chosen if he could have had his way.

After his outing to the theatre with Isobel, Geoff had come back late—or rather, early that morning—from Edinburgh. Fiona had heard the sound of Isobel's car dropping him off and when he had appeared at breakfast, he had had an abstracted, far-away look in his eyes, replying to her questions about the play with a vague lack of interest. By all appearances, Geoff was clearly a man whose thoughts were elsewhere.

His thoughts were with Isobel Carstairs, Fiona guessed, watching him hurry through his breakfast and then, when she told him that she was going riding, take himself off in the direction of Melrose. But with her disturbing and still completely baffling encounter with Ian on her mind, she had no inclination to involve herself in Geoff's romantic tangles. Let Ian and Geoff resolve their rivalry over Isobel themselves. She had reconciled herself to that, but what really hurt was that her husband should accuse her of deception, especially when the only deception she was practising was keeping, locked in her unhappy heart, the secret of her feelings for the man who had accused her.

It was a deception that her unwilling husband would applaud if only he knew, Fiona thought bitterly later that same day, when she was getting ready for the County Ball. She smoothed the folds of her long dress and regarded herself critically in the mirror in her room. She had bought the dress for her graduation from university the year before. Then it had seemed ideal because it had to be worn under her cap and gown, but now it seemed too plain, too schoolgirlish even, for the glittering evening ahead. Plain ivory silk with a pintucked bodice gathered into a simple waistline, its classic flow made her look even taller than ever, she decided sourly, unimpressed by the red-gold aureole of her hair and the supple lines of her slender body, but it was the only long dress she had and it would have to do. She turned away from the mirror, conscious that Geoff would probably already be waiting for her downstairs with only Janet's stony silence for company.

'Wow!' Relief and admiration mixed were written on Geoff's face when Fiona opened the kitchen door. 'You look fabulous! I'll be the envy of every man there!'

'Thank you.' Geoff was really doing a pretty good job of hiding his regret that she wasn't Isobel, Fiona thought, smiling her gratitude in spite of herself.

'Here, let me help you with your wrap.' Geoff bustled round her.

'You'll be back late then, I suppose.' Janet's chilly tones successfully extinguished the small flame of anticipation for the evening that had begun to grow.

'Not too late,' said Fiona. 'I daresay that by midnight we shall both be pleased to come home.'

When they arrived at Blackwoods, even Fiona's spirits had to improve. It was as though, somewhere on their rather subdued drive over, they had crossed an invisible barrier into another world. They had left Craighill in an atmosphere of sombre darkness, but Sir Archie and Lady Douglas's home was ablaze with activity and light. People streamed from the car park that had been marked out in the grounds into the huge vaulted entrance hall, where the shields and scabbards of Sir Archie's long-dead warring ancestors went way up in rows towards the shadows of the roof. Beneath them, and beneath the age-old tattered banners, everything was luxury and anticipation for the evening ahead. Heavy crystal and silver reflected in the gleam of overhead chandeliers and the exotic scent of out-of-season flowers, rising from the hothouse blooms banked around the newel posts at the foot of the great carved oak staircase, hung like incense in the air.

Standing in the receiving line waiting to greet her host and hostess, Fiona noticed with a burst of confidence that she was not the only woman to be simply dressed. This, it seemed, was one occasion when the men were the peacocks and their women-folk a subtle foil for their magnificence. With very few exceptions, Geoff among them in his formal dinner jacket, the men were in the kilt, and the reds, blues and green of Scotland's proud heritage swirled in front of Fiona's eyes with all the iridescent colours of a bubble as a lone piper in the minstrels' gallery played a reel.

Some of the women wore the plaid over their simple ball gowns; a length of material in the tartan of their clan worn sash fashion over one shoulder, with the long fringed ends floating as they danced. Apart from a flashing regret that she had not thought to wear the tartan of her own family, Fiona was suddenly completely pleased that she had come.

Perhaps for a few hours this scene of gorgeous un-reality would take her mind away from all the prob-lems still waiting to be resolved at Craighill. With a smile of genuine anticipation for the evening ahead, she stepped forward to take Lady Douglas's kid-gloved hand.

'So pleased you could come!' After a few brief words of greeting, Lady Douglas passed Fiona on to her husband standing next to her.

'So pleased ye could come!' Sir Archie repeated the formal greeting, but his glance was more curious. Unlike his wife, this was the first time that he had seen the new young neighbour whose arrival had set everyone by the ears in that normally un-eventful stretch of the Border.

'Thank you.' Fiona returned his glance with equal curiosity. Sir Archie was a wisp of a man ap-pearing considerably smaller than his stately wife, but in spite of his sixty odd years, he was wiry and strong and Fiona found herself being irresistibly re-minded of old Sim. There was also no doubt where Sir Archie had chosen to spend all his life. Unlike some of the richly plummy voices around them, his dry tones owed nothing to England or to an English boarding school education.

'It's guid to have someone from Craighill wi' us,' he said, increasing the pressure on Fiona's hand. 'Your uncle was not a great one for socialising, but many's the hour we've spent rapping in front of that great kitchen range of his—aye, and ridden out wi' the hounds as well. And who's this wi' ye?' he added abruptly. 'Don't tell me that we're going to have a wedding as well as a new neighbour at Craighill?'

For one incredible moment Fiona thought he knew, but then she realised that his eyes had darted past her to fix on Geoff standing by her side—and it was Geoff and not Ian that he had in mind as her husband.

She blushed. 'Oh, no,' she said. 'This is Geoff Gilson—I mean, may I introduce Mr Geoffrey Gilson. He's a friend I knew in London before I came up here.'

'I see.' In spite of her denial, Fiona had the uncomfortable suspicion that Sir Archie had still read more into her words than she had intended, and she was relieved when the bottleneck that their conversation had caused in the receiving line saved them from further questioning.

After a few words with Geoff, Sir Archie released them and they moved on into the crowded ballroom. Fiona's uneasiness subsided. What did it matter if Sir Archie chose to spread a rumour of the impending marriage of the new heiress at Craighill with a young man from London? Even if Ian heard, he would probably be pleased. When he had time to consider the situation he would realise that if she wanted to marry Geoff it would be one less obstacle in his own pursuit of Craighill and Isobel.

Geoff stopped in the doorway, studying the dancers on the packed floor. Taking advantage of his sudden preoccupation, Fiona too let her eyes roam across the scene, trying to convince herself that she was not really looking for the one person she half longed, half feared, to see.

Those few quiet seconds were the last she was to have that evening to contemplate the future. She had not realised how much interest her unexpected arrival had caused in the area and, after a first dance with Geoff, she went from one pair of arms to another, dancing until her feet ached and her lips were stiff with the effort of smiling and responding to politely inquisitive questions.

She was standing in the doorway to the supper room, catching her breath after a particularly hectic eightsome with Sir Archie, when the whole tenor of the evening dramatically changed. Her host had gone to get them both a glass of champagne and when she heard the sound of approaching footsteps, she half turned, a smile of thanks already forming on her lips. The smile froze and faltered when she saw to whom the footsteps belonged.

'May I have this dance?' The question had become routine, but this time it made Fiona's heart leap into her throat. And yet why should she be so surprised to see him? Her husband was as much a part of the life of the Borders as she was herself, and furthermore, he had been born there. It was perfectly natural that he should be at the County Ball.

Fleetingly aware of Sir Archie, a few feet away, halted in mid-stride with their champagne glasses in his hands, Fiona steeled herself to look her husband fully in the face, and for a few moments they could have been alone. Her whole attention was arrested by the man who had the right to use her as his wife.

He looked incredibly handsome—tall, dark, the brilliant scarlet of his dress Hamilton kilt and plaid glowing like fire against the velvet blackness of his silver-buttoned jacket and the white ruffles at his wrist and throat throwing the arrogant lines of his face into startling relief.

He was smiling, no different from anyone of the other young men who had asked her to dance, but, unlike the look of polite enquiry in their eyes, his held the glint of some cold, private anger that was completely alien to the occasion going on around them. Without waiting for an answer, he took her into his arms, holding her close with a grip that was outward silk but inward steel, forcing a response to the lilting rhythm of the small band that had taken the place of the piper who had played the eightsome reel.

For the first few steps Fiona found herself following his movements with a grace and fluidity that surprised her and, in the moments before he spoke, before the heavy lashes lifted and the slate grey eyes bored down into her, it would have been so easy to imagine herself telling him that she loved him and dream that she heard herself being told that her love was returned.

The first note of his voice dispelled all such

fantasy. He was still smiling for the benefit of the crowds surrounding them, but his smile only served to intensify the chill in the softly spoken words.

'I see that you have once more chosen to disregard my advice,' he said, nodding across the room to where Geoff was dancing with a tall, fair-haired girl.

A small remnant of the pride that had buoyed her up on so many occasions since she had arrived at Craighill came to Fiona's rescue.

'How can I disregard something when I haven't the slightest idea what you mean?' she retorted.

'In that case, I must be more explicit,' Ian replied smoothly. 'As I told you last night, I've had enough of games, and if you don't ask Mr Geoffrey Gilson to leave Craighill, I shall!'

As if to emphasise his words, he tightened his grip with an unconscious force that made Fiona wince.

'Come now, my dear Fiona,' he drawled, noticing. 'Smile! Surely you don't want all these good people to think that you're not enjoying yourself in their company, do you?'

'You have no right to tell me what to do!' Fiona hissed up at him.

'On the contrary,' he replied urbanely, smiling a greeting in the direction of a passing couple, 'if you will reflect a while, you will recall that I have every right!' The steel that was in his eyes entered his voice and chilled the air between them. 'Although circumstances may prevent you using it, you bear my name. As my wife, you have the right to my protection, and in return, I expect obedience.' He forestalled her protest with a mirthless laugh. 'Oh, I know that in this day and age obedience is not regarded as one of the wifely virtues, but in coming to Craighill, my dear Fiona, you have stepped into the past. We live by the old ways here and a man has the right to expect obedience from his wife. Obedience and respect!'

'Respect!' Fiona fairly spat the word. All the resentment about Isobel came boiling to the surface of her mind. Quite unconcerned about the curious glances that were beginning to be shot in their direction, she raised her voice. 'Respect! You of all people to use that word to me! Even at Craighill, respect is something that has to be earned—old Sim has taught me that at least! And with what you've done, how do you think I could ever respect you?'

Ian looked down at her. 'Maybe you're right,' he said at last, enigmatically. 'Maybe it will take time before you can respect me, before you can understand why I chose the course I did. But for the time being, you will most certainly obey me, and unless you want your guest to have a few very unpleasant moments indeed, before he finally goes on his way, I would suggest that you consider what I've said very carefully indeed. Maybe then you'll ask Mr Geoffrey Gilson to leave!'

Seething with inward anger but rendered speechless by his arrogance, Fiona had no option but to let the man she both loved and hated continue to lead her in the dance. A slight commotion at the entrance to the ballroom gradually distracted her attention. She craned her neck and, as if on cue, the dancers partially obscuring her view moved to one side and a small figure, dressed in vivid emerald green, sprang into sudden prominence, poised like an exotic humming bird on the shallow landing at the foot of the great stairs.

Isobel!

The clinging lines of the low-cut chiffon dress which should have made her seem garishly overdressed on this occasion of masculine brilliance only served to emphasise Isobel's blazing attraction, and Fiona knew that hers were not the only eyes to turn in the direction of the stairs.

Finally, satisfied with the impression that her late entrance had made, Isobel stepped forward to take Lady Douglas's hand. A smooth brown head, easily identifiable as Geoff's, had begun to forge its way across the crowded floor when a sudden instinct made Fiona look up. Ian's eyes were riveted on the scene being acted out in front of them.

Had there been any doubt in her mind before, the reason for his angry ultimatum was now crystal clear. For once it was not just the need to possess Craighill that drove him. He wanted Geoff away so that he could also have complete possession of Isobel.

CHAPTER NINE

BLUE FIRE cantered steadily across the turf and Fiona had only the task ahead of them in mind. They had been seventh in the dressage the day before and now the stiffest test of all in the three-day event about to come: the cross-country section. The first fence rushed towards them—a tricky post and rails. Over and away, to a thin spattering of applause from the line of spectators.

There was a right-handed turn downhill, and then they gathered momentum towards the Irish Bank. The mare lifted herself easily to the top of the solid obstacle, sure-footed like a cat, changing stride to slither down the other side and then away again, this time left-handed, towards the simple brush hurdle that would land them on the road.

Fiona heard the pounding rhythm of their gallop as they approached. It was fast—too fast. She fought to check the mare but, caught up in the heady excitement of this new experience, spurred on by the applause drifting after them in the light May breeze, Blue Fire resisted, throwing up her head against the pressure of the reins. At this rate she would never see the fence, Fiona thought, and it was fixed. Behind the deceptively harmless screen of brushwood, the top rail was solid, fixed to the uprights. One touch and they would be down—down on to the backbreaking hardness of the road beyond.

A pause, a check, and Fiona felt the mare make a supreme effort to lift them over the obstacle which she had seen too late. A crack as a hind leg touched and then—nothing. Just a whirling, eddying darkness taking her down in ever decreasing circles towards oblivion.

She fought for consciousness, struggling against the delirium that must be overtaking her when she imagined that she saw Ian's face hovering close to hers. That was impossible. Ian was at Craighill; she doubted if he even knew or cared that she was at Peebles. Geoff had come to the horse trials with her. Kind, infatuated Geoff, reluctantly leaving Isobel behind out of a sense of duty but talking of nothing else on the drive each day.

When Fiona woke, her first thought was that she must be under water. The air was moist and humid and the light had a curious greenish quality. She lay there, puzzled, until her fingers touched the iron frame of a canvas cot and she realised that she must be in the first aid tent. Attracted by the faint movement, the figure sitting at her side rose and bent over her, an indistinct blur to her slowly focussing eyes.

'No, don't move!' It was Geoff's voice.

An irrational sense of disappointment welled up inside her, ending in the two large tears that trickled slowly down her cheeks.

'How's Blue Fire?' she whispered, the thought of what might have happened to the mare making the tears fall in earnest.

'She's O.K.—really!' Geoff told her anxiously. 'A bad fall and a few bumps and bruises no doubt, but Sim says she's fine. He's taken her home in the horsebox: said to tell you that he'll call the vet from Craighill.'

Relief made Fiona cry harder and Geoff produced a large white handkerchief and began dabbing ineffectually at her cheeks.

'There now,' he said, his face crumpling in a mixture of embarrassment and sympathy. 'There's no need to cry. You'll both be right as rain in a few days, and cantering round the estate as if nothing had happened!'

'But before then, we're taking you to the Infirmary for a few X-rays, young lady!' The doctor in attendance at the trials had come up unnoticed beside them and the crisp efficiency in his voice was strangely comforting. He laid a cool hand on Fiona's forehead.

'I don't think there's any more than a very slight concussion and bruising,' he said, 'but we won't take any chances.'

It was dark by the time they got back to Craighill. Fiona had refused to stay overnight in the Infirmary, insisting on going home to see Blue Fire, but by the time Geoff drew up in the yard, she had to admit that the effort of walking even the few steps to the stable was too much for her. Filled to the brim with pain-killing drugs, her body a mass of slowly developing bruises, there was no pain, but her head was floating inches away from her shoulders.

Her riding boots had gone, taken off in the Infirmary, and Geoff had had to carry her out of the casualty department. He leaned forward now, waiting for her to link her arms around his neck, before lifting her easily out of the passenger seat of the car. The kitchen door opened, spilling light out into the dark yard, the fleeting movement of a shadow no more than a figment of Fiona's fevered imagination. Then Janet was there, and all the resentment that had been aroused by Geoff's arrival forgotten in concern.

Geoff had telephoned ahead, forewarning her of Fiona's accident, and the tiny housekeeper clicked her tongue anxiously as they moved into the light and she saw the pale face resting wanly on Geoff's shoulder.

'You'll take the poor lassie to her room at once,' Janet instructed firmly. 'I've some good warm broth on the stove and I'll be up with it directly to undress her and put her to bed. You'll not put a finger on her yourself!' she added sharply to Geoff's departing back as he began to carry Fiona up the steep flight of stairs leading from the kitchen to her room. 'My old mother would turn in her grave if she so much as heard of such a thing. A man in a lassie's bedroom, and an unwed lassie at that!'

Her voice faded away into a distant murmur of disapproval as they turned the corner on to the landing at the top of the stairs. Geoff laughed, a comfortable rumble in his chest against Fiona's cheek.

'I hardly think her mother has cause for concern wherever she may be, do you?' he asked.

Fiona shook her head. The slight movement disturbed the mass of cotton wool that filled it and she relaxed gratefully against the pillows as Geoff gently lowered her on to the bed. A lamp was burning and a fire had been lit and she lay, letting her eyes wander round the familiar contours of the room while a great feeling of warmth and tiredness gradually stole over her.

'.... unless, that is, you'd rather I didn't?' Geoff was talking to her, she dimly realised.

'Didn't what?' The distant voice that she produced with such great effort could not possibly be her own, Fiona thought.

'Stay with you,' Geoff explained. 'Would you like me to stay with you for a while?'

Fiona lay back and considered his suggestion. It was one that clearly needed a lot of concentration before she came to a decision. She looked across at him, surprised at the remarkable clarity with which her mind was suddenly functioning. She could see every detail of the room and of Geoff, but he was small, as though she was looking at him through the wrong end of a telescope. Her bedroom must have grown in size, she decided, letting out a long sigh as her eyelids irresistibly closed.

A brilliant shaft of sunlight forcing its way through a chink in the curtains and falling like a spotlight on her face awoke her. Her mouth felt dry, her head ached abominably and the drug-induced euphoria of the night before had completely disappeared. Every bone in her body ached and the weight of the bedclothes pressed down unendurably. Even the flimsy fabric of her nightdress was a burden against her legs.

A grunt and the sound of heavy movement from the big wing chair beside the now dead fire caught her attention. That part of the room was still in shadow, but she could see the top of a dark head resting awkwardly against the top of the chair. Ian! He was her first thought, and a quick flow of joy coursed through her. Somehow he had found out about her accident and had cared enough to come and sit the night through with her.

Every muscle in her body shrieking out a protest, Fiona levered herself up to see more clearly. The figure in the armchair moved again. A sleep-crumpled face appeared around the corner of the wing and a pair of blue eyes blinked drowsily at her. Disappointment drowned out all her aches and pains as she realised that it was Geoff and not Ian who had kept watch on her.

'Hi!' Geoff grinned, stretching his arms up above

his head. 'So you're awake. How are you feeling?'

'Not too bad!' Fiona resisted the temptation to take out her disappointment. After all, it was hardly Geoff's fault that he was not the one person in the world that she had hoped to see.

Geoff looked at his watch. 'Goodness,' he exclaimed, 'I must have been more tired than I thought!' He went on talking as he got up and drew the curtains. 'That little housekeeper of yours will have my head if she sees the state this room's in! I had a battle royal anyway to get back in here last night after she'd put you to bed. The only reason she finally gave in was because I promised to keep the fire alight and try and get you to take some more of her "good broth, ye ken!"' Geoff managed a surprisingly good imitation of Janet's sharp treble and Fiona laughed, stopping abruptly as an acute pain caught her ribs.

'Hurts, eh?' Geoff said sympathetically. 'Well, I'll just clear this away and go downstairs and call the doctor. They seemed to think there was no harm done yesterday, but it wouldn't hurt to have a second opinion.'

He came to the bedside table and picked up a tray containing a half emptied bowl of congealed soup. Fiona looked at it distastefully.

'Ugh!' she exclaimed. 'What are you going to do with *that*? Not try and get me to eat it, I hope!'

'Hardly—I had enough trouble getting that much into you last night! All you wanted to do was talk, and then you passed out on me in mid-spoonful! Do you remember?'

Fiona cast her mind back. She could remember Geoff lowering her on to the bed and she could now remember being woken up again as Janet had undressed her, but after that everything was blank. She must have had slight concussion, she supposed —and people in concussion sometimes said more than they intended, she realised sharply.

'I can't remember much—but what did I talk about?' she asked carefully.

'Oh, this and that.' Geoff stopped at the door, tray in hand, and looked at her. 'You know, my dear Fiona,' he said quietly, 'if it weren't for the fact that you're "prostrate on your bed of pain", I should say that there's a lot going on in that pretty head of yours that you haven't told me about and, as your resident father confessor, I should demand an explanation.' He noticed her stricken expression and reached for the doorknob. 'Oh, don't worry,' he added, 'I shan't pry. Just as long as you know that I'm very fond of you, Fiona, and there's nothing I wouldn't do to make you happy.'

He opened the door as he spoke and Fiona froze as she saw Ian outside, his hand upraised to knock. Ian did not move, but his eyes told her everything she needed to know about his thoughts. They flicked from the crumpled bed to her own stricken face against the pillows, and then across to Geoff's shirt-sleeved appearance. When Geoff finally saw him, even he was at a loss.

Ignoring Geoff completely, Ian spoke only to his wife. 'I came to see if you were all right,' he said contemptuously, 'but I can see that I needn't have bothered.'

With one last withering look, he spun on his heel and strode off down the passage to the front of the house. For once Geoff had no words. He could only shrug and smile apologetically as he closed the door, leaving Fiona to wrestle with the certain knowledge of what had been in her husband's mind: that in spite of all her denials, she and Geoff were lovers.

Janet arrived with her breakfast, insisting on feeding her as if she had been a child. The local doctor came and pronounced her fit enough to get up whenever she wanted. The sound of a car going down the drive announced Geoff's departure for Melrose and Isobel, but through all this, Fiona could think of only one thing—the look on Ian's face when he had seen Geoff leaving her room early that morning.

If only she could explain! Ian might have no interest in her, but it was desperately important that he should know that she had not been lying when she had told him that there had been no one in her life before she had agreed to marry him. Although it had bruised her body and had led to this terrible mischance, her fall seemed to have cleared her mind and she could see the web of coincidence and misunderstanding that had woven itself so closely around them as clearly as if it had been hanging in front of her on some morning hedgerow.

The yearning that had been growing inside her ever since that first night at Craighill, when her terror at the sound of unknown footsteps had been dispelled by Ian's totally unexpected appearance in the circle of light cast by the car's headlamps, returned to engulf her with full force. She could carry out her promise to leave Craighill. She could go back to London or even to the other side of the world. She could marry and have children but never, ever, would she experience the same sharp pang of longing that threatened to engulf her each time she saw the man who was her husband.

She sighed. For all her sudden insight, the distance between them remained impassable. She was his wife and yet they might have been hostile strangers.

Too weak to leave her room that day, she stayed in bed, alternating between bouts of wild optimism and tearful depression, but the following morning she knew that she was on the mend. With Janet's help, it was possible to get up and dress. Her body no longer throbbed with pain and she ate her breakfast with an appetite that surprised her before she went out into the barn to see Blue Fire.

The mare was standing, head down, back humped, the picture of dejection, but she pricked her ears at the sound of Fiona's voice and stretched her lip sensitively to take the proffered lump of sugar.

'There you are, old girl!' Fiona smiled as the sound of munching filled the improvised stable. The mare's spirits might be low, but there was nothing wrong with her appetite.

'There's nothing wrong wi' her except that she's ashamed o' hersel'!' Sim's voice at her shoulder made Fiona jump, but Blue Fire merely shifted with a rustle of straw.

'I didn't hear you come in, Sim,' said Fiona. 'What do you mean, she's ashamed of herself?'

'Ashamed o' hersel' for rushing her fences like some great loon without a bit of notice o' yersel' on top! I was watching, you understand,' the old man explained. 'Ah, well, she'll not do it next time,' he finished confidently.

'Next time?' At that moment, with Fiona still feeling the effects of their fall, climbing on to the mare's back seemed as unlikely as flying to the moon.

'Aye,' Sim went on imperturbably. 'You'll be wanting her to ride in a day or so, no doubt.'

She was so accustomed to taking Sim at his dour face value that it was a second or two before the slight twinkle at the back of his eyes dawned on her.

'Sim, I do believe you're teasing me!' she said incredulously.

'Aye, well, mebbe I am.' Sim's shy grin gave his face a curiously lopsided look as though the muscles had become stiff with disuse. 'But for all that,' he went on, 'I've not seen a body take a fall so bravely since the old laird used to hunt with the Perthshire. You're a true Montrose, lassie, there's no doubt about that!'

Embarrassed at having said so much, he stumped off, muttering to himself under his breath. Blue Fire moved across her stall, watching him go.

'Well, would you believe it?' Fiona said to the dapple grey rump. 'I've been accepted at last! I almost had to break my neck to do it, but I'm a Montrose at last!'

Sim's acceptance, small point though it was, filled her with an inspired sense of optimism and courage. With Sim's example to show the way, was it possible that she could also persuade Ian to see her in a different light? It would take all her newly awakened courage, but could she sweep away all the misunderstandings and jealousies that separated them and make her marriage work?

On their wedding day, Ian had called her 'beautiful and desirable'. She had repulsed him. Could he ever think of her like that again? Was it possible to make him understand that she had rejected him not because Geoff was already her lover but because of pride and later fear that he was using her not just to secure Craighill but to secure it against the day when he would once more be free to marry Isobel?

The thought of Isobel brought its usual wave of jealousy, but Fiona fought it down. She could not afford to be jealous if she wanted to achieve her aims. In spite of everything, she still only had the tiny divorcee's word on top of her own fevered imaginings that Ian actually wanted to marry Isobel. True, she had seen him take her into his arms that night outside the factor's lodge, but then Isobel had given him no choice. In her panic over Bowser's menacing pursuit, Isobel had flung herself into his arms, arousing a protective response that would have been automatic in any man. Then, to Fiona's knowledge, they had quarrelled and, true to her angry threat, Isobel had found another man. She had found Geoff, who was clearly bewitched by her.

Perhaps there was still a chance. Fiona's hopes soared, only to collapse once more. Before she could even speak to Ian, she must find a way of persuading Geoff to leave Craighill. Ian would never listen to her while Geoff was still living at Craighill.

Absorbed in her thoughts, Fiona had started off across the yard and Bowser had jumped up in his usual undisciplined way before she even realised that he was there. But where Bowser was, Geoff would not be far behind. The big dog had been so delighted by his master's arrival that he rarely left his side. Fiona disentangled herself and looked up. Sure enough, Geoff was just coming into the yard. She hurried towards him.

'Where's the fire?' Geoff asked.

'What? Oh, nowhere!' Fiona smiled. 'I was coming to find you, as a matter of fact!'

'And I was coming to find you! I've just seen that

buyer chap from Fingals off and everything seems to be under control. He'll be back in a couple of weeks when the painters have left to supervise hanging the curtains and laying the carpets. Now, how are you feeling?'

'I'm fine!'

An awkward air of hesitation settled between them. Underneath his normally good-natured air, Geoff was looking rather depressed, Fiona thought.

'And how are you feeling?' she asked.

'Oh, I'm fine, too,' Geoff replied, forcing a smile. Silence descended again.

'I wanted to ask you something.' In a way of ending such silences, they both spoke together and then laughed, their easy friendship returning.

'Well, ladies first!' said Geoff.

'No, visitors first. I insist!' Fiona replied.

'All right, then.' Geoff placed his hands gently on her shoulders. 'There aren't many people I could tell, but I know I can trust you, Fiona. I'm afraid I've made rather a fool of myself.'

The look that Fiona had noticed a few seconds earlier returned to his brown eyes.

'I'm sure you haven't,' she said reassuringly. 'But what's happened? Why do you think you have?'

'It's Isobel. She....' Geoff faltered, and Fiona's hackles rose. Wherever she went it was Isobel. Whether it was her husband, or Geoff, or whoever, every man she knew seemed prepared to dance to Isobel Carstairs' tune.

'What about Isobel?' she asked sharply, regretting

it the moment she spoke. Her angry response had made Geoff look even more drawn.

'She's gone. I went into Melrose first thing this morning, before that buyer chap from Fingals came, and her uncle told me that she's just packed up and left.'

Isobel gone! Fiona felt as if life had just given her a present. If Geoff had not looked so cast-down and might not have misunderstood her motive, she could have kissed him. Isobel had been the one big obstacle in her way to Ian, but now, if what Geoff said was true, that obstacle had been removed.

'But why?' she asked, wondering suddenly if Isobel's departure might not be part of another scheme to tantalise Ian and come back later with even more effect.

'She's got the offer of a modelling job in America, apparently,' Geoff told her.

'Isobel, a model?' said Fiona, surprised.

'It's something to do with a man she met when she was still married, her uncle said,' Geoff explained. 'Someone on the motor racing circuit. Did I tell you that her husband was a racing driver among other things?' he enquired. 'Well, presumably this man said that if ever Isobel needed a job she was to contact him. She did, and he somehow fixed her a work permit and she flew to America from Prestwick airport this morning.'

'Without telling you?' Fiona said sympathetically.

'Oh, well, I suppose you can understand it. The

chance to be a top model in New York doesn't come every day.'

'Dear Geoff, Fiona thought. He was always willing to see the best in everyone. Some day he would meet a girl who really was the best.

'Anyway,' he went on, 'what I wanted to tell you was that I've decided to go back to London.'

'But you've still got some more holiday left!'

'I know.' His grin held a hint of his old good-humoured self. 'But I have the feeling that you'd rather I didn't spend it here. No!' He forestalled Fiona's protest with a wave of his hand. 'You're forgetting that I spent a night with you!'

'You what?' said Fiona, appalled. Had Isobel's departure deranged Geoff's mind?

He laughed.

'The night of the three-day event, remember?' he said. 'If you don't, I do! And if you also remember, I told you the following morning that you talked a lot in your sleep!'

Fiona looked at him quickly. She had wondered how much he had heard that night he had sat up with her. Apparently he had heard too much.

'Yes, I know about your marriage,' Geoff told her, 'and I think Hamilton's right for you, Fiona. And I also think that if he's half the man I suspect he is, he'll prove it. I'm not saying that, at one time, when I came up here, I wasn't hoping ... well, that I wasn't hoping that one day you would be Mrs Geoffrey Gilson, but I knew from the moment I arrived that I hadn't got a chance. And since that night, since I heard you talking in your sleep, I know why I was too late. I also know that while I'm here, I'm causing problems for you. That's why Bowser and I have come to say goodbye.'

Hearing his name, the big dog jumped up.

'You're going now, this morning?' asked Fiona.

'Well, there's no point in waiting, is there? Who ever gained anything by waiting? Perhaps that's what you should go and tell that husband of yours!'

Ten minutes later Bowser was climbing into the passenger seat of Geoff's car and Geoff was off down the drive with a final wave of his hand as he accelerated towards London and whatever life had in store for him.

Fiona watched him go with mixed feelings. On the one hand she felt regret and a lingering concern about how he would fare, on the other, an almost lightheaded relief that his departure confirmed the absence of Isobel and left the way clear for her attempted reconciliation with Ian.

She went back into the house. Since the arrival of the decorators it had been completely opened up and Janet was bustling across the hall in the direction of the main staircase.

'Have you any idea where Mr Hamilton is?' Fiona asked.

'He'll mebbe be in the office,' Janet replied tartly, flicking at an invisible speck of dust on the banister with her duster. 'Though how a body can be expected to keep track of all the comings and goings in this house, I don't know. To say nothing of keeping everything clean!' she added pointedly.

'Oh, don't worry. We'll see if a girl from one of the farms will come in and help you.' Fiona was already on her way to the office, a conversation about the problems of housekeeping the last thing she wanted. If she was ever to confront Ian, she knew that she must do it now, before her courage failed.

Determined though she was, when she got to the farm office door she stopped, unwilling to knock and yet reluctant to go in unannounced. She was being foolish, she told herself. Whatever her motive for being there, she was still mistress of Craighill and as such had the right to go anywhere she chose.

She turned the heavy brass handle and eased the door open. The room was empty. Ian had been there, the disarray of papers on the desk proved that, but there was no sign of him now. An exaggerated sense of anti-climax swept over her. She had been so sure, so confident, that before the day was over all the misunderstandings that separated them would have been swept away.

The only thing she could be sure of was that he would not be spending that evening with Isobel. Unless, of course, the fair Isobel had changed her mind and decided not to go to New York after all.

Fiona's heart skipped a beat, but the more she thought about it, the more certain she was that Isobel would not change her mind.

However much Isobel might have set her sights on becoming mistress of Craighill, and however much she might have flirted with Geoff in an attempt to make Ian jealous, New York was a new world, and a person like Isobel would always be tempted by new worlds to conquer.

She had a job as a model and the chance to be independent and admired. This would give her what she had always wanted, and the elegant divorcee would be the first to recognise the wisdom of the old saying that a bird in the hand was worth two in the bush.

Fiona realised that her own arrival at Craighill had been a great blow to Isobel's ambitions as far as Ian was concerned. Geoff was an eligible bachelor, but he also had a mind of his own. The price of marrying Geoff would have been a life spent travelling the remote parts of the world as the wife of a hardworking construction engineer. New York offered glamour, a career in her own right.

No, Fiona decided as she started to climb the stairs to her room, she had nothing to worry about on Isobel's account, but she would do well to worry about herself.

The next morning, delayed reaction to her fall and to the emotional upheaval that had followed it set in again. She was content to stay in bed and let Janet fuss over her like an anxious mother hen. The feeling of confidence that had filled her the previous day had evaporated, leaving her weak and uncertain of her ability to convince Ian and to shear her way through the wall of suspicion and misunderstanding that separated them.

She could not even be certain about his feelings for her. Even though Isobel had gone, it did not follow that she held any more than a physical attraction for him, Fiona thought. His moments of love-making had always been passionate, violent even. He had never shown her the tenderness that she had seen him capable of with Isobel.

The day slowly passed, and in the periods between waking and sleeping she again began to long to turn her back on her inheritance and go back to London to the lonely, uncomplicated life she had left behind.

The telephone call from Aunt Madeline came late that afternoon.

Janet fairly ran into Fiona's room.

'Hurry, Miss Montrose! Hurry!' she exclaimed, the thought of the money ticking away at the end of the long-distance line too much for her thrifty soul to bear.

Unwillingly, every bone in her body aching a protest, Fiona slipped on her dressing gown and went down to the front hall to take the call. It was chilly standing on the stone-flagged floor and she shivered slightly as she picked up the receiver.

'Hallo, hallo!' Aunt Madeline's reedy voice was coming querulously down the line. The connection must be good if she was ringing from her villa in Spain, Fiona thought.

'Of course I'm not in Spain,' her aunt said sharply a few seconds later when Fiona asked. 'I'm in London! That fool doctor of mine insisted that I should come back for a check-up. Not that it's done any good—my arthritis is just as bad as ever and this nursing home is costing me a fortune. That's why I telephoned.'

'You want to come up here?' Fiona asked, surprised.

'Of course I don't want to come up there!' Madeline said firmly. 'The last thing I want to do is come traipsing up to the wilds of Scotland. But I do want to get back to Spain as soon as I can and it seems little enough to ask that I should see my only relative before I go. I want you to come down here tomorrow, because I'm going home the next day!'

Fiona thought how typical it was that, with absolutely no notice at all, she should be expected to travel down to London, but at least she owed her aunt that much for all the years of duty that had gone into her upbringing, she supposed. Having got her way, Madeline rang off and Fiona slowly replaced the receiver. The sun outside looked good compared to the chilly shadow of the hall and she made her way out to the front entrance. Going to London would mean delaying her confrontation with Ian until she came back, she realised.

Like magic, the sun soaked into her bones and

took away their ache. She looked out over the shrubbery towards the moorland vista, greening now with the approach of high summer, and wondered what London would be like after all these weeks in the peace and quiet of the Scottish countryside. But unless she pulled herself together and telephoned for a taxi to take her to the station the following morning, she would never find out.

She made her call and was halfway across the hall towards the stairs, gathering her thin robe about her, when the green baize door leading to the kitchen opened and swung to and the sound of footsteps striding towards her found an echo in the thumping of her heart. Her mouth went dry. She knew without turning to whom the footsteps belonged and her courage failed.

She waited to turn until Ian was right behind her, so close that if she had swayed she would have brushed up against him. The anger in his body reached out to her and she shuddered, frightened in spite of herself by the sheer masculine hostility in his eyes.

'So you can't even let a day pass before you have to make arrangements to go running after him!' His voice was harsh, matching the breath that seared her cheeks.

'I don't know what you mean,' she whispered.

'Oh, come now! "I don't know what you mean!"' he mimicked cruelly. 'I happened to pick up the extension in the kitchen, woman! I heard you. I heard you on the telephone making arrangements to go to London to be with your lover!' He spat the word with contempt.

A sudden anger equalling his own flooded through Fiona and the pride of the Montroses was in her as she threw back her head and met his eyes, her auburn hair aureoled in the sunlight now streaming in through the cathedral window over the stairs.

'*My* lover!' She laughed mirthlessly. '*My* lover! *You* can say that after all the nights I've listened for the sound of *her* car to leave your cottage! You have the gall, the effrontery to——'

A loud crash from the landing above them halted the rising tide of fury that threatened to engulf her. She looked up. One of the painters on his way home had been attracted by the sound of their angry voices and had stopped to listen. He grinned apologetically, stooping to retrieve the empty bucket that had fallen from his hands.

Ian shrugged his shoulders and nodded meaningfully, in the direction of the hall. 'Let's go.' The hand he placed on her shoulder was outwardly casual, but it had an inward grip that made Fiona catch her breath.

'Go where? We have nothing to talk about.' Determined to show no pain, Fiona kept her voice low for the benefit of their audience, but the anger was still surging and rolling like a stormy sea inside her.

'And I say we have!' This time he even smiled,

but the grip on her arm remained firm, drawing her irresistibly across the hall towards the seclusion of the farm office.

Unless she wanted to make a scene for the benefit of the painter still on the landing above them, Fiona had no choice. She must go with him.

The rigidity of his arm forced her into the office ahead of him and he had kicked the door shut behind them with a heart-stopping finality before he swung her round to face him. There was no sign of anger now, just a mirthless humour that was far more threatening.

'Maybe you're right,' he said smoothly. 'Maybe we've passed the time for talk, but I've also had enough of playing games. You're my wife, and now I think I must teach you exactly what that means.'

He reached for her, passion flaming in his eyes, and as Fiona stepped back his hand caught in the neckline of her flimsy robe, wrenching it apart.

She caught her breath. This was her husband, the man to whom she longed to give herself, but with love, not fury. She had dreamed of passion, but with gentleness.

'You're quite beautiful,' he drawled, his look raking the body that she tried to cover with the remnants of the tattered cloth. 'And what's more, you're mine!'

Fiona retreated as he moved towards her, but the tiny office was too cramped. She had never been more aware of its isolation as he swept her up, helpless but still protesting, in his arms, and flung her down on the padded leather sofa with a force that drove the breath from her lungs.

She lay there, his moving shadow looming over her, reminding her that her female strength was too small to defy the onslaught of his masculinity. Words perhaps could save her.

'You promised,' she said breathlessly. 'You said that this was to be a marriage in name only!'

'I also said, my dear Fiona, that in coming to the Borders you'd stepped backwards in time. Here it's the man who decides when a woman must become a wife.'

He stood above her, muscled sinew, light reflecting from the smooth sheen of his skin. She rose up to defy him, but his hands forced her back, no gentleness in their touch. She fought, but he laughed, lips curled back in a mirthless smile.

Then his hands, his arms, his mouth were upon her and her skin burned under the rising tide of passion that mounted to engulf them both. Finally she surrendered and her wild cry brought peace, lying in his arms, wife in reality as well as name.

CHAPTER TEN

THE sky had grown dark before Ian left. Crushed, humiliated and yet uniquely alive as she was, it was a long time before Fiona found the strength to gather her robe about her and follow him more slowly out of the gloomy little office. She had heard her husband go striding off out of the front of the house and it was with relief that she turned in the opposite direction and made her way up the back stairs to the refuge of her room.

The mixed emotions that he had aroused in her were still with her on the train the following morning as she journeyed to London to keep her appointment with Aunt Madeline. She knew that there was a strong streak of the untamed running through Ian's nature. She had experienced it last night. She had experienced it before in the merciless grip of his fingers on her arm. There was the memory of that half-strangled sob with which he had finally torn himself away and left the room.

Had it not been for that one choked exclamation, she would have thought that the whole episode had been nothing more than an act of revenge for the loss of Isobel. But the sob had held a thousand words, not all of them harsh or angry or punishing, and the gentleness that had also been there with him after his first burst of angry passion made it impossible for her heart to believe that he had been only eager for vengeance.

Sitting in the railway carriage with the country-side slipping quickly past to the iron rhythm of the wheels, Fiona quelled her heart. This time she would listen to her head. She would have to go back to Craighill to settle up all the business of the estate, but she must never go back expecting to find either happiness or fulfilment as the wife of Ian Hamilton. What more did she need to make that plain? He had used his strength and her weakness to demon-strate once and for all that he was to be the sole master at Craighill. He had punished her and now he had finished with her. If he had not, surely she would have seen some sign of him that morning before she left? Surely he would not have let her go without a single word of explanation or regret?

It was late in the day before the train arrived in the busy London railway terminus. It was too late, Fiona thought, to stop and book herself into an hotel. If she was to see Aunt Madeline at all that afternoon, she would have to go straight to the nursing home.

The discreetly expensive medical establishment in which Aunt Madeline was having her annual check-up was in Kensington, no more than a stone's throw away from the mews cottage that Fiona had rented from Geoff when her aunt had sold up so suddenly and gone to Spain. The cottage where even now Geoff was deciding on his future, Fiona supposed, as she paid off the taxi and went up the steps to the nursing home's front door.

Although it was barely early evening, Aunt Madeline was already in bed. She looked surprisingly small sitting up against the oversized pillows, much smaller and more frail than Fiona remembered from their last meeting less than a year before. The hands that were lying on the coverlet seemed more twisted with arthritis and the sudden surge of affection, mixed with compassion, that overcame Fiona as she looked at her only living relative made her hurry across the room and kiss the faded cheek —the first kiss that they had exchanged in years. For a second, the elderly woman looked surprised, but Fiona could see that she was pleased, and momentarily regretted all the opportunities for affection that had been missed over the years.

'You're not looking as well as I expected!' The months might have aged her, but Aunt Madeline's voice still held the same slightly critical and austere note that had greeted Fiona's arrival at Hatchways as a seven-year-old orphan and had made her burst into tears.

Now she was older and quite used to the tone. 'I had a fall,' she explained, going on to describe the accident with Blue Fire that had brought them both down on to the bone-shaking hardness of the road.

Typically, her aunt offered no sympathy. 'That

mare needs a man to ride her,' she said, 'I told you often, but then you never were one for taking much notice of what you were told! Learn by experience —that was your motto, even as a child—just like your father! And what about this other piece of foolishness of yours? Insisting against the best advice on hanging that great white elephant round your neck and going and burying yourself in the country just because you had some idea about finding your roots. Roots! Pah!'

Aunt Madeline snorted and Fiona remembered the highly discouraging letters that had passed between them when she had written telling her aunt about her surprise inheritance and her aunt had written back strongly advising her to sell.

'You'll be regretting it now, I daresay!' Madeline added sharply.

'Oh, no, I've no regrets.' Thinking at first only of Craighill and everything that the house and land had come to mean to her, Fiona replied with a shining fervour, but even half way through that simple sentence the thought of Ian, never far beneath the conscious surface of her mind, came back to grasp her and she faltered. Her eyes fell and her voice became tremulous and uncertain. Aunt Madeline's eyes were by no means distracted. Sharp as ever, they peered at the girl she regarded as her niece, but when she spoke her voice was smoothed with a note of understanding that Fiona had rarely heard before.

'So that's it!' she breathed. 'And where is he?

Down here in London or back at Craighill?'

'He?' Totally surprised, Fiona struggled for pretence. 'I don't know what you mean,' she said.

'Your father could never get round me when he was a boy, and neither can you, my girl! There's a man somewhere—I know it! You're forgetting that I've seen you after too many falls to be deceived by some story about a riding accident. Oh, I daresay you've had that as well.' She raised a misshapen hand as Fiona started to protest. 'But no riding accident ever gave a woman the look you've got on your face!' The voice, the eyes, the smile were marvellously soft and sympathetic. 'You can tell me, you know—you're not the only person to have trodden the same path. Others had gone before.'

Tempted to confide, Fiona hesitated. She had realised that Aunt Madeline would have to be told one day about her marriage and the reasons for it, but the last thing she had intended was that she should be told now. But even while she hesitated, she began to speak, and the whole story, nothing left out or neglected, came pouring out for the first time to ears other than her own.

In some strange way, during the telling she must have been drawn towards the high, nursing home bed because, when she was about to finish, she realised that she was sitting there, her hands held in those of her aunt, comforting and warm.

'I'll have to leave, of course,' Fiona said. 'I can't see any other way. And maybe if I leave and go right away, one day I'll forget. One day, I'll wake up and realise that I haven't thought of Ian for days, weeks, months—that I've forgotten what it was to really be in love. Maybe I shall even be able to smile about it all!' She bit her lip, strangely calm now that her decision was made, as if the tears she felt along her cheeks belonged to someone else.

'Don't ever do that!' Aunt Madeline spoke with an intensity and her fingers gripped with a force that Fiona would not have guessed that they possessed. 'Don't ever let love fade until it becomes something to be smiled at in the years to come! Oh, you'll smile all right, I daresay, the human spirit will see to that, but even while you're smiling you'll hurt and wish and long that the years could roll back and you had the choice to make again. Go back, girl—now! Tonight! There's still time for you to be on the night train.'

The crippled fingers disengaged themselves and the urgent power in her aunt's voice was such that Fiona was on her feet before she realised the impossibility of what she was being commanded to do. It *was* impossible! She could never face Ian now. Not now. The fantasy of his gentleness that she had dreamed of on the train had been no more than that. He had wanted to take revenge for his loss of Isobel. He had taken it, and he would never expect her to approach him again.

'I can't!' Her voice was no more than a desperate whisper.

The tired figure in the bed drew herself up and

Fiona braced herself for the tirade. Always unexpected, Aunt Madeline beckoned.

'Come and sit down,' she said. Drawn by the compulsion in the old woman's eyes, Fiona obeyed and felt her hand once more taken up by fingers whose touch transmitted more than words with a living force. 'Once I was like you,' Madeline went on in a voice that had somehow become younger. 'Once I was in love with a man called Hector.' The grip of crippled fingers forestalled Fiona's sudden start of incredulous surprise. 'My parents took me to visit cousins who lived in a great house on the Borders. The younger boy, James, was no more than a boy, but Hector was a man and I loved him. I loved him and he loved me, but somehow we never got round to telling each other. Oh, it wasn't dramatic or anything like that, no forbidding parents or threats of disinheritance, but in my young day people weren't as frank and open about their feelings as they are nowadays and we just never talked about it.' She paused, filling in with thoughts everything that the words had left out. 'Oh, years and years later—when that husband of yours was a skinny, dark little boy of about ten with a temper like the devil—I went back to Craighill for curiosity's sake. But by then it was too late. Hector had changed and so, I suppose, had I——' she gave a reminiscent, sad smile. 'And do you know, we laughed! We laughed about those two young people who had been so painfully and secretly in love all those years before. It was the most unhappy moment of my life. Don't——' The fingers tightened until Fiona almost cried out. 'Don't ever let that happen to you.'

For a second her aunt really looked like the young girl in the faded photographs in her great-uncle's room. The young girl in the straw boater and frilly, high-necked blouse, always standing next to Sir Hector and once, it seemed, with her hand through his arm.

'Go back, Fiona.' Madeline's voice was old now and tired but it had lost none of its inner force. 'Go back and fight for what you really want. Lose in battle, but never, never lose by just going away!'

Fired by the compulsion in the voice that she had been taught to obey when she was a child, Fiona was at the door before she realised the impossibility of her aunt's demand. She turned, leaning back against the wall, her hands outstretched in a gesture of defeat.

'I can't go back, Aunt Madeline,' she whispered.

'Then this will be the first time,' came the sharp retort. 'I've never known you give up so easily before. Time and again you'd fall off your first pony when you were a girl and there was never any question of giving up then. You had to be dragged away from the saddle before you'd stop. That's another thing you have in common with your father—you fight for what you want. You always have!'

'But this is different, can't you understand!' Fiona's voice rose in a desperate attempt to convince the implacable small figure propped up against the pillows in front of her. 'We're not talking about a wayward child trying to control a pony. We're talking about me as I am now and about the man who is my husband. You've not seen the look on his face, heard the contempt in his voice. I love him, yes! I need him, yes! But I'm not going back. You call it giving up, but I call it accepting the truth. Ian Hamilton doesn't want me as his wife. He's never wanted me for his wife, and I'm not going back to beg!'

There was a pause, broken only by Fiona's heavy breathing. Aunt Madeline regarded her silently.

'Well, if you won't, you won't,' she said eventually. 'You're wrongheaded and you're a fool, but if you've made up your mind, I know better than to persuade you. And what, if I may ask, do you propose to do now?'

'I don't know. I just don't know!'

'Well then, as a start, you can come and see me off at the station.'

'What?' Her aunt's abrupt change of subject caught Fiona off balance.

'You can be at Victoria Station tomorrow when my train leaves,' Madeline said firmly.

Why not? Fiona thought. She would have to go back to Craighill eventually to settle up the business of the estate, but it would be a few days before she could face up to that. Meanwhile, there was no reason why she should not see her aunt off on her long overland journey through France to Spain.

In fact, although Aunt Madeline mistrusted flying, there was no reason why Fiona should not catch a plane and be in Spain to meet her when she arrived.

'Rubbish!' Aunt Madeline would have nothing to do with the idea. 'I like my peace and quiet and I've no desire to have you mooning around. No, my girl, you've made your decision and you stick by it. You stay in London. There's no future for you in Spain keeping an old woman company!'

'I could come to the nursing home tomorrow, though, and drive to the station with you,' Fiona suggested.

'Oh, dear, when will you learn to do just what you are asked?' Madeline said wearily. 'If the inefficiency of the staff here so far is anything to go by, I'll have quite enough to do getting myself and my belongings to the station on time. The last thing I need is to have you here to bother about as well. No, you be at the station, my girl. It will be nice to have you there.

'Twelve should be time enough,' she went on. 'Under the clock at Victoria Station just before noon tomorrow.'

Fiona smiled and stooped to kiss the faded cheek.

'Under the clock just before twelve,' she agreed. 'Goodnight, Aunt Madeline. Sleep well.'

'Hm!' Madeline snorted, 'I doubt I shall be sleeping at all until I get back into my own bed!'

CHAPTER ELEVEN

FIONA climbed into a taxi and gave the name of the old-fashioned family hotel to which Aunt Madeline had always taken her when she had been a child, up on a visit to London from the country.

The hotel had not changed, Fiona thought, thirty minutes later. Much though her own life might have altered, it was still the same as it had always been. She had even been given the room overlooking the busy thoroughfare of Piccadilly that she remembered sharing with Aunt Madeline. Then she had been eager to defy her aunt and hang out of the old sash windows looking down at the crowds below. Now the sight saddened her. It was a fine evening and there were many couples strolling along the pavements taking advantage of the pleasant air. Fiona watched until her heart caught in her throat. One man was so like Ian—tall, dark, his arm caressingly around the waist of a young, auburn-haired woman who could have been Fiona herself.

As if sensing Fiona's interest, the man glanced up and the illusion was immediately dispelled. He was no more her husband than she was the girl at his side.

She turned away from the window, unwilling to

see more. She was alone, just as she had been before she went to Scotland and just as she would be until she could dissolve this marriage of love on her side and contempt on his and put all thoughts of Ian Hamilton aside.

In part she wished she could have followed her aunt's advice and gone back to Scotland to fight for her marriage, but what was the point? He could not have made it more clear that he despised her.

There was just one second when his look had said that he was claiming her as his wife, but then he had left her, Fiona harshly reminded herself. He had left her, in the little room that had been Sir Hector's study, without one word of explanation or regret. Nor had he taken the trouble to see her before she had left Craighill for London early that morning.

The crowds swirled round Fiona as she waited at Victoria Station the following morning. She had not slept well, her mind beset by thoughts of Ian, re-tracing again and again all that had happened during her eventful visit to Craighill. It seemed only yesterday since that rainy evening she and Bowser had arrived at Craighill, but how much had happened in the meantime. How well she could remember that first meeting with Ian as he opened the door and his first words—'You'll be Miss Montrose.' Even then, she now realised, Ian had done something to her heart. There had followed that unforgettable ride with him when he had first shown her Craighill. 'The best way to see Craighill is on horseback,' he had said, and he had been right. But it was Ian riding by her side that she remembered more than Craighill. The warm feelings engendered that day had not lasted long, she recalled, as she thought of the city-bred Bowser chasing the sheep and Ian's blazing anger, 'After yesterday, I would have thought you would have had more sense! You're on a farm now—or had you forgotten!' There had followed his unromantic proposal of marriage and her equally unromantic acceptance— 'I'll marry you to save Craighill, but as a business arrangement, nothing more.' Ian had never known she was already in love with him, that she really wanted much, much more from him than a marriage of convenience. Tradition had demanded that he be at her side, as her estate manager, when the presentation of the new mistress of Craighill to the tenants had taken place. He was by then also her fiancé, but he had seemed even more distant as if to underline the purely business nature of their agreement. She thought of her wedding day—so different from the wedding day she had always envisaged, but nevertheless unforgettable because she had been marrying Ian. Was it all to become just a memory? Was Ian to become to her with the passage of time the same as Hector had become to Aunt Madeline? No, that was impossible—not after all that had happened between them. She thought of that last passionate scene with Ian and his words,

'Here it's the man who decides when a woman must become a wife!'

Her thoughts in a turmoil, she glanced momentarily up at the ornate clock. It was now nearly twelve and there was no sign of Aunt Madeline. It was most unlike her aunt to be late. Fiona's eyes narrowed as she looked across at the departure board. It seemed to her that the white figures said that the next boat train left at four. There must be some misunderstanding; Aunt Madeline could not have made such a mistake. She stared at the indicator in disbelief.

'Going somewhere?'

A very familiar voice broke into her thoughts and she spun round. It couldn't be! Ian was standing there.

For one breathless moment they stared into each other's eyes, and then they were in each other's arms. For an instant, Fiona had the wild impression that he had been expecting her, and then everything was lost as the firm hard strength of his body enfolded her and his lips brushed her hair, their soft touch contrasting with the fierce, possessive pressure of his grip.

This could not be happening. One moment she had believed she had lost Ian for ever, the next she was in his arms. If the touch of his fingers had not been so real, she would have known she was dreaming.

Gradually he released her, holding her at arm's

length as if to reassure himself that she was really there.

'What—what are you doing here?' In spite of his kisses and her longing to respond, Fiona forced herself to speak calmly and hold herself erect. She had been hurt too much and did not dare believe the inner sense that told her he had come in search of her.

He had come to London to look for Isobel, she told herself. He could not know that Isobel had already gone to America.

'I came to talk to you. Although the middle of a busy station hardly seems the best place to do it.' For the first time, a gleam of humour lit up the grey eyes.

'But what have we got to talk about?' Fiona asked. 'And how did you know I'd be here?'

'Your aunt telephoned last night and told me.'

'Aunt Madeline?'

The sudden shriek of a train whistle reminded Fiona that she had come to the station to say goodbye to her aunt. She looked quickly at the departures board.

'Oh, don't worry. Your aunt left hours ago,' said Ian. 'She's a very exceptional woman—in case you didn't know.'

'But I'm here to say goodbye to her!' Fiona explained. 'She told me that her train left at twelve.'

'That, my darling——' for a few moments, he was silent, looking into her eyes, '—was to give me time to fly down from Scotland. Your aunt, in fact, left on an early train.'

'But I don't understand——' Fiona was in a turmoil.

'Your aunt telephoned me last night,' he explained. 'She told me everything you talked about. I'd thought I'd lost you, but she said that if I came down to London there was still a chance that you would come back with me to Craighill as my wife. So here I am.'

'Your wife?' She felt she must be dreaming until she looked into his eyes and felt the intensity of her response as he swept her up into an endless kiss.

'Do you believe me now?' he asked eventually, tilting her head with one long finger under her chin and with a look in his eyes which made her heart turn over. 'Do you believe I want you as my wife?'

The light in her eyes gave him her answer. 'Let's go home,' she said.

Supper was over on their first night back at Craighill and Janet had gone. They were alone together. Fiona thought the lamplight gave Ian's face an unusually gentle look as he patted the arm of the old laird's chair in its place beside the brightly polished kitchen range and drew her down beside him. She nestled up against him and he hooked a finger through the gold chain on which she wore her wedding ring around her neck.

'You haven't told me yet,' he said quietly, 'but

will you be wearing this now, Mrs Hamilton?'

'Oh, yes—I will!' Fiona repeated her marriage vows in the two sighed words, but there was still one thing to be exorcised to make her happiness complete.

'What—what about Isobel?' she asked.

'And Gilson?' Ian smiled, squeezing her hand. 'Aunt Madeline told me everything. I've not seen Isobel since the night of the County Ball,' he told her. 'I understand she's gone to New York—I was told she's got the offer of a modelling job from some man she met. Isobel always had an eye for the main chance.'

'But her car was always parked outside your house, night after night,' she protested.

'Her car may have been outside, but she wasn't inside. She wasn't staying far away, you know—and that's a typical provocative Isobel ploy.'

'Yes, I suppose you could call her provocative,' Fiona agreed drily.

Ian grinned. 'Have you ever walked into a cobweb?' he asked. 'It's so soft and fragile and yet you can't get rid of it. However much you pick off, there's still more there, clinging and tenacious. Well, that was Isobel—a delicate, clinging, steel cobweb.'

'With an eye for the main chance!' Fiona reminded him.

'Aye, well, I suppose you can't blame her. Just divorced and suddenly finding a man on his own who is apparently about to inherit a fortune.'

'To say nothing of the fact that she's a very attractive woman.' Fiona could not resist the gibe.

In answer, Ian raised her face to meet his softly mocking eyes.

'You know,' he said, 'I've always thought a little jealousy a very becoming fault in a wife.'

His lips were still on hers as, with one easy movement, he lifted her in his arms and carried her effortlessly through the door and up the back stairs to her room. The hardness in the strong masculine body that had once possessed her was in total contrast to the delicious weakness flooding through Fiona's limbs. Even if she had wanted to, there could have been no resistance, and now her longing to prove herself his wife was part of that desire.

He flung open the door to her room and stood looking down at her. She lay in his arms, silvered in the moonlight streaming through the window, the deep plunge of her dress disclosing the first swelling curve of her breasts.

'I knew you were beautiful,' he whispered passionately. 'What I can't believe is that I now know that you're mine!'

The shadows moved in the darkened corridor behind them and there was the sound of a sharply indrawn breath of disbelief.

'If my old mother could have lived to see this day,' Janet said, 'she would have turned in her grave!'

JOY
ROMANCE
LOVE

Harlequin Omnibus

THREE love stories in ONE beautiful volume

The joys of being in love . . .
the wonder of romance . . .
the happiness that true love brings . . .

Now yours in the HARLEQUIN OMNIBUS
edition every month wherever
paperbacks are sold.

And there's still *more* love in

Harlequin Presents...